Culture & Leisure Services
Red Doles Lane
.... .d. West Yorks HD2 1YF

D0506302

"Do you usually flirt with women you think are pregnant?"

"There's no guy to stop me from moving in on you."

This time she had to chuckle—in spite of herself. "I was just thinking…you might be a card-carrying good guy. If I were ever going to trust a doctor again—which I'm not—it might have been you."

"I'd ask you out…but I'm afraid if we had a good time, you'd quit disliking me, and then where would we be?"

She lifted her head and kissed him.

Her lips. His lips. Like a meeting of whipped cream and chocolate. Not like any kisses, but the "damn it, what the hell is happening here?" kind.

She pulled back and looked at him.

When he got his breath back, he said, "Do we have any idea why you did that?"

"I've been known to do some very bad, impulsive things sometimes."

"So that was just a bad impulse." He shook his head. "Sure came across like a great impulse to me."

Dear Reader,

I had enormous fun writing this story!

For one thing, I rarely take on a heroine with a temper—a real temper—and Ginger gave me a run for my money when she let loose.

And then there's Ike, who's determined to believe he's a laid-back, easygoing kind of guy…when he so isn't.

En route, I had to visit a tea farm for research—this was *really* tough, sampling all those wonderful teas, seeing the eagles close up and having the chance to meet the owners of this extraordinarily special place.

There's also a character named Pansy in the book…I have no idea where she came from, but once she showed up on the page, she refused to be ignored.

This is Ike's story—the second book about the MacKinnon family—and I hope you love it as much as I loved writing it. Don't hesitate to write me through my web site, www.jennifergreene.com, any time you want to pop in!

All my best,

Jennifer Greene

The Baby Bump

JENNIFER GREENE

First published in Great Britain 2013
by Mills & Boon, an imprint of Harlequin (UK) Limited.
Large Print edition 2013
Harlequin (UK) Limited,
Eton House, 18-24 Paradise Road,
Richmond, Surrey TW9 1SR

© Alison Hart 2013

ISBN: 978 0 263 23764 1

Harlequin (UK) policy is to use papers that are natural, renewable and recyclable products and made from wood grown in sustainable forests. The logging and manufacturing process conform to the legal environmental regulations of the country of origin.

Printed and bound in Great Britain
by CPI Antony Rowe, Chippenham, Wiltshire

JENNIFER GREENE

lives near Lake Michigan with her husband and an assorted menagerie of pets. Michigan State University has honored her as an outstanding woman graduate for her work with women on campus. Jennifer has written more than seventy love stories, for which she has won numerous awards, including four RITA® Awards from the Romance Writers of America and their Hall of Fame and Lifetime Achievement Awards.

You're welcome to contact Jennifer through her website at www.jennifergreene.com

To "my" librarians
at the Benton Harbor and
St. Joseph libraries. From the start,
you encouraged me to write and
nourished my writing dreams.
You've always gone out of your way
to help everyone in the community
enrich their worlds through books.
You're the best!

Chapter One

Back when Ginger Gautier was a block-headed, reckless twenty-one-year-old, she'd have taken the mountain curves at ninety miles an hour and not thought twice.

Now that she was twenty-eight…well, she couldn't swear to have better judgment.

Unfortunately she was eight weeks pregnant—by a doctor who'd claimed he deeply loved her just a day before he bought an engagement ring for someone else. So. Her judgment in men clearly sucked.

She'd lost a job she loved over the jerk. That said even more about her lack of good judgment.

Some said she had a temper to match her red hair. Friends and coworkers tended to run for cover when she had a good fume on. So possibly her temper might be considered another character flaw.

But she loved.

No one ever said that Ginger Gautier didn't give two hundred percent for anyone she loved.

When she passed the welcome sign for South Carolina, she pushed the gas pedal a wee bit harder. Just to eighty miles an hour.

Gramps was in trouble. And she was almost home.

The eastern sky turned glossy gray, then hemmed the horizon in pink. By the time the sun was full up, Ginger had shed her sweater and hurled it in the backseat on top of her down jacket. When she left Chicago, it had been cold enough to snow. In South Carolina, the air was sweeter, cleaner, warmer…and so familiar that her eyes stung with embarrassingly sentimental tears.

She should have gone home more often—way more often—after her grandmother died four years ago. But it never seemed that simple, not once she'd gotten the job in hospital administration. Her boss had been a crabby old tyrant, but she'd loved the work, and never minded the unpredictable extra hours. They'd just added up. She'd come for holidays, called Gramps every week, sometimes more often.

Not enough. The guilt in her stomach churned like acid. Calling was fine, but if she'd visited more in person, she'd have *known* that Gramps needed her.

The miles kept zipping by. Another hour passed, then two. Maybe if she liked driving, the trip would have been easier, but nine hundred miles in her packed-to-the-gills Civic had been tough. She'd stopped a zillion times, for food and gas and naps and to stretch her legs, but this last stretch was downright grueling.

When she spotted the swinging sign for Gautier Tea Plantation, though, her exhaustion disappeared. She couldn't grow a weed, was never engrossed in the agricultural side of the tea business—but she'd worked in the shop as a teenager, knew all the smells and tastes of their teas, could bake a great scone in her sleep, could give lessons on the seeping and steeping of tea. No place on the planet was remotely like this one, especially the scents.

Past the eastern fields was a curve in the road, then a private drive shaded by giant old oaks and then finally, finally…the house. The Gautiers— being of French-Scottish origin—inherited more ornery stubbornness than they usually knew what to do with. The word "plantation" implied a graceful old mansion with gardens and pillars and maybe an ostentatious fountain or two. Not for Ginger's family.

The house was a massive sprawler, white, with no claim to fanciness. A generous veranda wrapped around the main floor, shading practical rockers and porch swings with fat cushions. Ginger opened the door to her Civic and sprang out, leaving everything inside, just wanting to see Gramps.

She'd vaulted two steps up before she spotted the body draped in front of the double-screen doors. It was a dog's body. A huge bloodhound's body.

She took another cautious step. Its fur was red-gray, his ears longer than her face, and he had enough wrinkles to star in a commercial for aging cream. He certainly didn't appear vicious…but she wasn't positive he was alive, either.

She said, "Hey, boy" in her gentlest voice. He didn't budge. She cleared her throat and tried, "Hey, girl." One eye opened, for all of three seconds. The dog let out an asthmatic snort and immediately returned to her coma.

For years, her grandparents had dogs—always Yorkie mixes—Gramps invariably carried her and Grandma usually had her groomed and fitted up with a pink bow. The possibility that Gramps had taken on this hound was as likely as his voting Republican. Still, the dog certainly looked content.

"Okay," Ginger said briskly, "I can't open the door until you move. I can see you're tired. But it doesn't take that much energy to just move about a foot, does it? Come on. Just budge a little for me."

No response. Nothing. Nada. If the dog didn't make occasionally snuffling noises, Ginger might have worried it was dead. As it was, she figured the big hound for a solid hundred pounds...which meant she had only a twenty-pound advantage. It took some tussling, but eventually she got a wedge of screen door open, stepped over the hound and turned herself into a pretzel. She made it inside with just a skinned elbow and an extra strip off her already frayed temper.

"Gramps! Cornelius! It's me!"

No one answered. Cornelius was…well, Ginger had never known exactly what Cornelius was. He worked for Gramps, but she'd never known his job title. He was the guy she'd gone to when a doll's shoe went down to the toilet, when she needed a ride to a party and Grandma couldn't take her. He got plumbers and painters in the house, supervised the lawn people, got prescriptions and picked up people from the airport. Cornelius didn't answer her, though, any more than her grandfather did.

She charged through, only taking seconds to glance around. The house had been built years ago, back when the first room was called a parlor. It faced east, caught all the morning sun, and was bowling alley size, stuffed to the gills with stuff. Gram's piano, the maze of furniture and paintings and rugs, were all the same, yet Ginger felt her anxiety antenna raised high. The room was dusty. Nothing new there, but she saw crumbs on tables, half-filled glasses from heaven knows when, enough dust to write her name on surfaces.

A little dirt never hurt anyone, her grandmother had always said. Gram felt a woman who had a perfect house should have been doing things that mattered. Still.

A little disarray was normal. Beyond dusty was another.

She hustled past the wild cherrywood staircase, past the dining room—one glass cabinet there had a museum-quality collection of teapots. A second glass cabinet held the whole historic history of Gautier tea tins, some older than a century. Past the dining "salon," which was what Gramps called the sun room—meaning that he'd puttered in there as long as she'd known him, trying samples of tea plants, mixing and mating and seeing what new offspring he could come up with.

The house had always been fragrant with the smell of tea, comforting with the familiar whir of big ceiling fans, a little dust, open books, blue—her grandma had had some shade of blue in every room in the house; it was her favorite color and always had been. Longing for Gram almost made her eyes well with tears again. She'd even loved Gram's flaws. Even when they had a little feud—invariably over Ginger getting into some kind of impulsive trouble—their fights invariably led to some tears, some cookies and a big hug before long—because no one in the Gautier family believed in going to bed mad.

The good memories were all there. The things she remembered were all there. But the whole downstairs had never had a look of neglect before. She called her grandfather's name again, moving down the hall, past the dining room and the butler's keep. Just outside the kitchen she heard—finally!—voices.

The kitchen was warehouse size, with windows facing north and west—which meant in the heat of a summer afternoon sun poured in, hotter than lava, on the old tile table. A kettle sat directly on the table, infusing the room with the scents of Darjeeling and peppermint. A fat, orange cat snoozed on the windowsill. Dishes and glasses and what all crowded the tile counter. The sink faucet was dripping. Dust and crumbs and various spills had long dried on the fancy parquet floor.

Ginger noticed it all in a blink. She took in the stranger, as well—but for that first second, all her attention focused on her grandfather.

He spotted her, pushed away from the table. A smile wreathed his face, bigger than sunshine. "What a sight for sore eyes, you. You're so late. I was getting worried. But you look beautiful, you do. The drive must have done you wonders. Come here and get your hug."

The comment about being late startled her—she'd made amazing time, he couldn't possibly have expected her earlier. But whatever. What mattered was swooping her arms around him, feeling the love, seeing the shine in his eyes that matched her own.

"What is this? Aren't you eating? You're skinny!" she accused him.

"Am not. Eating all the time. Broke the scales this morning, I'm getting so fat."

"Well, if that isn't the biggest whopper I've heard since I left home."

"You're accusing your grandfather of fibbing?"

"I am." The bantering was precious, how they'd always talked, teasing and laughing until they'd inevitably catch a scold from her grandmother. But something was wrong. Gramps had never been heavy, never tall, but she could feel his bones under his shirt, and his pants were hanging. His eyes, a gorgeous blue, seemed oddly vague. His smile was real. The hug wonderfully real. But his face seemed wizened, wrinkled and cracked like an old walnut shell, white whiskers on his chin as if he hadn't shaved—when Cashner Gautier took pride in shaving every day of his life before the sun came up.

She cast another glance at the stranger…and felt her nerves bristle sharper than a porcupine's. The man was certainly no crony of her gramps, couldn't be more than a few years older than she was.

The guy was sprawled at the head of the old tile table, had scruffy dirty-blond hair, wore sandals and chinos with frayed cuffs and a clay-colored shirt-shirt. Either he was too lazy to shave or was growing a halfhearted beard. And yeah, there was more to the picture. The intruder had tough, wide shoulders—as if he could lift a couple of tree logs in his spare time. The tan was stunning, especially for a guy with eyes that certain blue—wicked blue, light blue, blue like you couldn't forget, not if you were a woman. The height, the breadth, the way he stood up slow, showing off his quiet, lanky frame—oh, yeah, he was a looker.

Men that cute were destined to break a woman's heart.

That wasn't a problem for her, of course. Her heart was already in Humpty Dumpty shape. There wasn't a man in the universe who could wrestle a pinch of sexual interest from her. She was just judiciously assessing and recognizing trouble.

"You have to be Ginger," he said in a voice that made her think of dark sugar and bourbon.

"Aw, darlin', I should have said right off…this is Ike. Come to see me this afternoon. He's—"

"I saw right off who he was, Gramps." He had to be the man her grandfather told her about on the phone. The one who was trying to get Gramps to "sign papers." The one who was trying to "take the land away from him." Gramps had implied that his doctor had started it all, was behind the whole conspiracy, to take away "everything that ever mattered to him."

Ginger drew herself up to her full five-four. "You're the man who's been advising my grandfather, aren't you, bless your heart. And that has to be your dog on the front porch, isn't it?"

"Pansy. Yes."

"Pansy." For a moment she almost laughed, the name was so darned silly for that huge lummox of a dog. But she was in no laughing mood. She was in more of a killing mood. "Well, I'd appreciate it if you'd get your dog and yourself and take off, preferably in the next thirty seconds."

"Honey!" Her grandfather pulled out of her arms and shot her a shocked expression.

She squeezed his hand, but she was still facing down the intruder. "It's all right, Gramps. I'm here. And I'm going to be here from now on." Her voice was as cordial as Southern sweet tea, but that was only because she was raised with Southern manners. "I'll be taking care of my grandfather from now on, and we won't need any interference from anyone. Bless your heart, I'm sure you know your way to the front door."

"Honey, this is Ike—"

"Yes, I heard you say the name." She wasn't through glaring daggers at the son of a sea dog who'd try to cheat a vulnerable old man. "I really don't care if your name is Judas or Sam or Godfrey or whatever else. But thanks so much for stopping by."

He could have had the decency to look ashamed. Or afraid. Or something besides amused. There was no full-fledged grin, nothing *that* offensive, but the corners of his slim mouth couldn't seem to help turning up at the edges. "You know, I have the oddest feeling that we've gotten off on the wrong foot."

"You can bet your sweet bippy we have," she said sweetly.

"I strongly suspect that you'll change your mind before we see each other again. I promise I won't hold it against you. In fact, I'm really happy you're here. Your grandfather thinks the world rises and sets with you."

"Uh-huh." He could take that bunch of polite nonsense and start a fire with it. She wasn't impressed. She made a little flutter motion with her hands—a traditional bye-bye—but she definitely planned to see him out the door. First, so she could lock the screen doors after him, and second, to make darned sure he took the dog.

He was halfway down the hall when he called out, "Pansy, going home now." And the lazy, comatose, surely half-dead dog suddenly sprang to her feet and let out a joyful howl. Her tail should have been licensed as a weapon. It started wagging, knocking into a porch rocker, slapping against the door. Pansy seemed to think her owner was a god.

"Goodbye now," Ginger said, just as she

snapped the door closed on both of them and flipped the lock. Obviously, locking a screen door was symbolic at best. Anyone could break through a screen door. But she still wanted the good-looking son of a shyster to hear the sound.

She whirled around to see her grandfather walking toward her with a rickety, fragile gait.

"Sweetheart. I don't understand what got into you. You know that was Ike."

"I know, I know. You told me his name already."

"Ike. Ike MacKinnon. My doctor. I mean *that* Ike."

For the second time, she had an odd shivery sensation, that something in her grandfather's eyes wasn't…right. Still, she answered him swiftly. "You know what Grandma would say—that he can't be a very good doctor if he can't afford a pair of shoes and a haircut."

When her grandfather didn't laugh, only continued to look at her with a bewildered expression, she hesitated. She shouldn't have made a small joke.

The situation wasn't remotely funny—for him or her. Maybe she hadn't immediately recognized that Ike was Gramps's doctor—how could she? But she'd have been even ruder to him if she had known. Gramps had said precisely on the phone that the "doctor" was behind it all. Behind the conspiracy to take the land away from him and force him to move.

"Gramps, where is Cornelius?"

"I don't know. Somewhere. Chores. The bank or something." Her grandfather reached out a hand, steadied himself against the wall, still frowning at her. "Ike is a nice man, Rachel. And you've always liked him. I can't imagine what put you in such a fuss. I can't remember you ever being rude to a soul."

She stopped, suddenly still as a statue.

Rachel was her grandmother's name.

"Gramps," she said softly. "It's me. Ginger."

"O' course," he said. "I know that, you silly one. Next time, don't take so long at the hairdresser's, okay?"

She smiled at him. Said "I sure won't," as if his comment and her reply made sense.

It didn't, but since she was reeling from confusion, she decided to change gears. Gramps was easily coaxed to settle in a rocker on the veranda, and he nodded off almost before he'd had a chance to put his feet up. She was free then to stare at her car, which unquestionably was stuffed within an inch of its life.

The boxes and bags weren't heavy. She refused to think about the pregnancy until she was ready to make serious life decisions—and Gramps's problems came first. Still, some instinct had motivated her to pack in lighter boxes and bags. Of course, that meant she had to make a million trips up the stairs, and down the long hall to the bedroom where she'd slept as a girl.

The whole upstairs brought on another niggling worry. Nothing was wrong, exactly. She'd been here last Christmas, and the Christmas before, and for quick summer weekends. But her visits had all been rushed. She'd had no reason or time to take an objective look at anything.

Now…she couldn't help but notice that the whole second floor smelled stale and musty. Each of the five bedrooms upstairs had a made-up bed, just as when her grandmother was alive. The three bathrooms had perfectly hung-up towels that matched their floor tile color. But her grandparents' bedroom had the smell of a room that had been shut up and abandoned for months or more. Dust coated the varnished floor, and the curtains were heavy with it.

There was nothing interesting about dust, of course. As soon as you cleaned, the dust bunnies under the bed reproduced—sometimes doubled—by morning. Ginger had never met a housekeeping chore she couldn't postpone. It was just…a little dust was a different species than downright dirt.

The whole place looked neglected.

Gramps looked neglected.

When the last bag had been hauled from the car, her childhood bedroom looked like a rummage sale, but enough was enough. She opened the windows, breathed in the fresh air then crashed on the peach bedspread. She was so tired she couldn't think.

She was so anxious she was afraid of thinking.

In the past month, her entire life had fallen apart…which she had the bad, bad feeling she was entirely responsible for. She'd been bamboozled by a guy she'd lost her heart to, lost her job, shredded everything she owned to sublet her Chicago apartment, had a completely unexpected pregnancy that she had no way to afford or deal with…and then came the call for help from Gramps.

She'd fix it all.

She had to.

And Gramps came first because…well, because she loved him. There was no question about her priorities. It was just that she was getting the terrorizing feeling that her grandfather's problems weren't coming from without, but from within.

And if anyone was going to be able to give her a better picture of her grandfather's situation, it was unfortunately—very, very, *very* unfortunately—his doctor.

Chapter Two

Still yawning, Ike lumbered downstairs barefoot with the dog at his heels. Pansy had woken him, wanted to be let out. He opened the back door, waited. Pansy stepped a foot outside, stopped dead, let out a howl and barreled back in the house.

Ike peered out. There happened to be a snake in the driveway. A big one. A rat snake, nothing interesting.

"You live in South Carolina," he reminded Pansy. "You know about snakes. You just leave them alone. They don't want to hurt you. Just don't get in their way."

Pansy had heard this horseradish before. It hadn't worked then, either. She continued to dog his footsteps, closer than glue, all the way into the kitchen. He opened the fridge, peered in and had to shake his head.

He must have left the door unlocked again last night. The proof was in the white casserole on the top refrigerator shelf, tagged with a note from Maybelle Charles. The casserole was her mama's famous Chicken Surprise recipe. On the counter there seemed to be a fancy pie—pecan—anchored on hot pads that he'd have to return. The pie would definitely be from the widow five doors down, Ms. Joelle Simmons. The basket on the front porch held a peck of late South Carolina peaches. Babs, he suspected.

This was possibly the best place for a single man to live in the entire known universe. The whole town seemed to think he was too thin and incapable of feeding himself. The unmarried female population all seemed convinced that he needed a woman to shape him up. The more bedraggled he looked, the more they chased him. No one seemed to worry that he was a natural slob. They'd all decided, independently, that the right woman could fix minor male problems like that.

The food thing had started a day after he'd moved to Sweet Valley—which was more than three years ago. It was the same day he'd taken over old Doc Brady's country practice, the same day he'd found this fabulous ramshackle place just a couple blocks from the center of town. Come to think of it—it was even the same day his parents had expressed stunned horror that he'd failed to take a cardiac surgery option at Johns Hopkins, the way they had, the way any self-respecting MacKinnon was supposed to do. His two siblings had already failed their parents by choosing their own paths, but Ike had been the worst disappointment, because he'd actually decided to follow the family heritage of doctoring. Only he was never supposed to take a job here, in this bitsy town that could barely afford a doctor in the first place.

Everything about Sweet Water was perfect for him…except for the minor issue with all the food. The single ladies expected their plates returned. They cooked and baked and made everything on pretty little girly-type plates that invariably had their names on the bottom. Only when he returned them, he usually had to fight to leave.

He was bushwhacked into a chair, fed something else, made to drink something else, was expected to shell out some flirtation and interest.

Ike couldn't summon the energy to be rude, but he lucked out when Pansy showed up at his door. She refused to leave him, insisted on being adopted and went with him everywhere. She really helped with shortening the visits from all the single ladies.

Upstairs was home. Downstairs was his office—as in open to any and everyone.

Old Doc Brady hadn't run it that way, but Ike did. He'd inherited some help with the place. Bartholomew had some personality issues, but he cleaned the whole first floor at night and loved the part-time work. A retired nurse named Stephie still lived in the area, and always came in if he needed extra help. And the mainstay of the office was sixty-year-old Ruby, who was a wee bit bossy—but she could run a small country without breaking a sweat.

Right now, though, was his favorite time of day. He fetched a mug of coffee and the paper and ambled out to the screened-in back deck. Tuesday he had no scheduled patients until ten. Ruby would shout to let him know when she got there.

Pansy refused to come out. She was still worried about the snake.

Ike was worried about nothing. The morning was cool; he'd had to pull on a sweatshirt. Occasionally he heard the regular sounds of school buses going by, cars starting to congregate behind lights, stores opening and the occasional conversation as people headed for work or breakfast.

He'd finished the paper and started his second mug of coffee when he heard Ruby's voice from the front desk—and then the brisk snap of her footsteps coming down the hall to the back door. Par for the course, her portly shape was draped in a wild flower print, accessorized—her word, not his—by bright pink earrings, shoes and lipstick.

"Lady here to see you, Doc. Ginger Gautier. Cashner Gautier's granddaughter. You've got a ten o'clock—"

He glanced at his watch. It was only 9:10. "If you wouldn't mind, ask her to come on back."

"You mean in your office? Or in an examining room?" More than once, Ruby felt obligated to explain appropriate behavior to him, always tactfully and framed as a question. Still, her tone made it clear that patients shouldn't be seen on the back porch.

But Ginger wasn't a patient. And he knew what she'd come to talk about.

It was always a touchy situation when someone embarrassed themselves. It wasn't tough on the person who'd been the victim—him. But it was usually difficult for the person who'd done the embarrassing thing. Her.

As quickly as Ruby disappeared, he heard Ginger's lighter footstep, charging fast—Ike suspected she'd really, really like to get this meeting over with. From the open door, he could see her climb over the exhausted Pansy and step out onto the quiet back porch. She looked…

Delectable.

The hair was wild. Calling it red didn't explain anything. The color wasn't remotely ginger, like her name; it didn't have any of that cinnamon or orange. It was more like dark auburn, with a mix of sun and chestnut, with some streaks of red shivering in the long, thick strands. She'd strapped it up with some kind of hair leash. In the meantime, she had silver shining in her ears, on her wrist. Today she was wearing greens. A dark green shirt, pale green pants.

There was a lot of blue in those eyes. The same blue as a lake in a storm, deep and rich.

Her face was an oval. The eyes took up a whole lot of space, dominated everything about her face. She had thin, arched brows, gloss on her lips, but otherwise he couldn't tell if she wore any makeup. She had that redhead kind of skin, though…translucent, clear, clean…give or take the smattering of freckles.

As far as the body…well. She looked more

like the kind of girl you brought home to meet Mom rather than the kind a man imagined under the sheets. But Ike was nonstop imagining that body under the sheets right now. There was a lot of music, a lot of passion, in the way she moved, the way she did everything he'd seen so far. Of course, he'd been celibate for too long a stretch, so maybe he was dreaming up the sizzle he sensed in her.

That celibacy had probably been dumb. Abstinence had never worked well for him, and he could have slept with any number of ladies in town. Somehow he never had.

Maybe that was because no woman had really enticed him before. Not like Ginger seemed to. Heaven knew he could analyze her body for three, four hours and still want to analyze more. For one thing, she had significantly perky breasts. The breasts themselves weren't all that significant, but the perky was. They were round, firm, pressed just right against the shirt. She had no waist to speak of. But the pants—well, the pants begged to be taken off. They were just cotton, or some other lightweight fabric, but he could see the outline of her fanny, her thighs, her calves. She might be on the skimpy side, weight wise, but she looked strong and healthy, making it extremely easy to imagine her legs wrapped around him, without those pants. Without that blouse.

Damn, but she was refreshing. Challengingly refreshing. Even the resentment in her flash of a smile was disarming. He was getting mighty sick of women smiling at him as if he were slab of meat. Being disliked was a lot more interesting.

"I was hoping you'd come by to talk. Want some coffee?"

She nodded. "Black." She motioned to Pansy. "Does that dog ever move?"

"Rarely. About ninety percent of the day she's in a coma. But don't say the word d-i-n-n-e-r or there'll be hell to pay. And I'm talking relentless." He motioned her to a white Adirondack rocker while he stepped into the kitchen/lab, came back with a mug for her, and a fresh one for him. "How's Cashner doing today?"

"Happy as a clam." She locked her palms around the mug. "But I'm not. Being with him has made me scared to death."

He nodded. "I'm glad you came home."

"I had no idea. I talked to him on the phone—"

"All the time. I know. He told me. He thinks the sun rises and sets with you. And he holds it together in some conversations, especially in the early part of the day. He's always in good humor. Never a complainer. He can talk a blue streak, telling jokes, spinning yarns, talking about the tea farm. It's not always apparent to other people what's been going on."

"He told me…" She hesitated, and he guessed the apology was coming. Or the closest he was going to get to an apology. "He told me his doctor was trying to take the land away from him. Force him to move. That his doctor was behind the conspiracy."

"Yeah. That would be me. The evil doctor. Not about forcing him. That's not my place. But especially in the last couple months, I've been pushing him to believe he could live a lot easier in a place with more help."

"He doesn't want help."

"I know."

"He doesn't believe he needs help."

"I know."

"Last night I found him sitting in the wet grass. Wearing a suit. Around one in the morning."

Ike winced in sympathy.

"He calls me Ginger. And a minute later, he'll call me Rachel. My grandmother's name. And sometimes I'm Loretta. Do you have a clue who Loretta is?"

Ike shook his head.

"And then there's Cornelius. Cornelius was old

before I was born. Half the afternoon yesterday, they played cards. Rummy. And canasta. Cornelius was as balmy-headed as my gramps. Nothing's getting cleaned. Cornelius seems to make food sometimes. And forget other times…" At the sudden sound of voices coming from inside the house, she said immediately, "Do you have a patient? I know I should have called first, before stopping by."

"First patient's at ten. Ruby'll let me know when he gets here."

"Okay." She took a breath. "Listen, Doc—"

"Ike," he corrected her gently. "I'm your grandfather's doctor, not yours."

She immediately launched into an emotional sputter. "He was perfectly fine at Christmas and Easter both! He's been fine every darned time I call! I was here in *June* for Pete's sake. I don't understand how he could have changed so much, so fast!"

"Because that's how it hits people sometimes."

She launched into the next rocket round of nonstop sputter. "Well, what exactly *is* wrong with him—and *don't* tell me Alzheimer's. Or that there's nothing you can do. I want to know what tests you've run. If you've sent him to specialists. I may not have a heap of money, but my grandfather can afford the best of any kind of treatment. And I can stay here. I mean…I don't know how on earth I could find a job here. But for however long it takes, I can stay here, live with him. I could make sure he gets everything he needs, nutrition and medicine and exercise or whatever else you think he needs—"

"Ginger." He said her name to calm her. He was watching her face. She was so upset. Naturally. Who wouldn't be, to suddenly find out someone you loved had a fragile health issue? But there was something more going on. He'd seen her take a sip of coffee, and then immediately put the mug down. She'd had peach-healthy color in her cheeks when she came in, but that color was fading, her face turning pale.

Still, he answered her questions. "Yes, Cashner's been prescribed some medications that help a lot of people. There's no perfect medicine for this. I sent him to Greenville for tests, put him in the hands of two physicians I know personally. He's been tested and evaluated and retested."

"Don't you say it," she warned him.

He got it. She wasn't ready to hear the words *Alzheimer's* or *dementia.* "I'll give you the other answer," he said patiently. "Old age."

"He's not that old!"

Ike nodded. "I think it's possible he had some mini strokes a while back. He's been on high blood pressure meds from long before I came here. But he's at a point where I'm not certain if he remembers to take them. I set up a schedule for him, to help him remember, conveyed the same information to Cornelius. But sometimes—"

Ruby showed up in the doorway. "Doc. Mr. Robards is here. It'll take me a few minutes to get him weighed in and BP done and then into a gown, but then he's ready."

Ike started to say, "I'll be there in a minute," then noticed Ginger jump to her feet faster than a firecracker. Ruby's interruption had given her the perfect excuse to take off. She either wanted to get away from him, a depressing thought, or she needed to absorb what he'd told her about her grandfather. Alone.

Whatever her reasons, she stood up damned fast. The last pinch of color bleached from her face, and down she went. He barely had time to jerk forward, protect her head and help ease her to the ground. The porch only had matting for a rug.

Ruby rushed through the door, muttering, "Well, I'll be" and "What the sam hill is this about?" and then Pansy pushed through the door. Pansy invariably liked commotion. She jutted her jowly head under Ike's arm, trailing a small amount of drool on Ginger's hair. Ruby hunkered down just as intrusively.

"Ruby. Pansy. She needs air. And I need space."

Ruby took several creaking moments to get back to her feet. "I'll get a damp washcloth. And a BP unit."

"Good thinking. Thanks." He nudged Pansy out of the way, thinking that he'd been hoping to get his hands on Ginger—but not in this context. She was already coming to. Her eyes opened, dazed, closed again. She frowned in confusion—another sign that she was regaining full consciousness—and then she raised a hand, as if her first instinct was to sit up.

"You're fine, Ginger. Just stay where you are for a minute. It's just me. Ike."

No temp. He didn't need a thermometer to be certain. Normal color was flushing back into her face. He brushed his hands through her hair, feeling for bumps or lumps, any injury that might have caused the faint. He pressed two fingers on her carotid artery.

Accidentally, he noticed the rapid rise and fall of her breasts. The softness of her. The scent on her skin—not flowers, not for this one. Some sassy, citrusy perfume. It suited her.

Ruby hustled back with the BP unit. He took it, finding what he expected, that it was slightly on the low side. Again, he took her pulse as he studied her face. Her pulse rate was coming back to normal. And then, when her eyes suddenly met his, that pulse rate zoomed way out of the stratosphere.

Yeah. That was how he felt around her, too.

"If you need me…" Ruby said from the doorway.

"No. She's fine. Or she will be in a minute. Just give Mr. Robards a magazine and tell him I'll just be a few minutes, not long." He never turned his head. Focused his gaze only on her, tight as glue.

He knew a ton of women…but few with the fire of this one. Loyal. Passionate.

Interesting.

Her forehead crinkled in one last confused frown, and then she seemed to recover herself altogether. She muttered something akin to "Good grief" and pushed off the porch matting—or tried to.

He didn't forcibly hold her down, just put one hand on her shoulder. "I know you're getting up, but let's keep it slow."

"I'm fine."

"Uh-huh. You're pregnant, aren't you?" It was the doctor asking the question, but the man listening for the answer. Most of the time Ike didn't have to separate the two, but for this question, for this woman, he definitely did.

"Say what?" Wow. Those soft, sensual blue eyes abruptly turned glacier blue. Color slammed into her face. "What on earth made you ask that!"

He'd like her to think he was naturally brilliant, but the truth was it had just been a gut call, a wild guess. It was her response that gave away the truth of it. He answered slowly, "Just a short list of clues. Everything about you looks healthy and fit. You asked for coffee, but your hand shot to your stomach when you took a sip. Then you fainted out of the blue."

This time she pushed free and fast, got her legs under her, stood up. He watched for any other symptoms of lightheadedness, but saw nothing. "If you're diabetic, better tell me now. And are you on prenatal vitamins? Have anything prescribed for nausea?"

Okay. He'd pressed too far, judging from the sputter. The smoke coming from her ears. Her hands fisted on her hips. "Let's get something straight right now, Doc."

"Go for it." He eased to his feet.

"You're my grandfather's doctor. Not mine."

"Got it."

"My private life has nothing to do with you."

"Got it," he repeated. "But if you haven't been on prenatal vitamins—"

"What is it about small towns? People leap to conclusions over a breath of wind. No one said I was pregnant. No one has any reason in the universe to think that."

"So there's no guy." He just wanted to slip that question in there, while she was still talking to him.

"Exactly. There's no guy."

"I wondered," he admitted.

Ouch. She was shaking mad now. "For the record—" She punctuated her comments with a royal finger shake. "—I wouldn't fall for a doctor if he were the last man in the country. On the continent. On the entire planet…."

"Got it," he said again. "I'm sure glad we had this conversation."

That was it. She spun around, stepped over the dog, yanked open the back porch screen door and charged down the hall. Ruby peeked her head out of exam room one—then snapped her head back, clearly alarmed at getting in Ginger's way.

Ike followed her exit—mostly by following the swing of her fanny and bounce of her hair—all the way to the slamming of his front door.

Ruby popped her head out again. She didn't speak. Just raised her eyebrows.

Ike shook his head. "Don't ask me what that was."

But Ginger lingered in his mind. He was so used to being treated like a catch.

So many single women in the area fawned over him. Played up to him. They'd been spoiling him rotten, with food and attention and God knows all kinds of subtle and less-than-subtle offers.

It was a nice change of pace to meet a shrew. She was such a breath of fresh air.

He blew out a sigh, headed inside to wash his hands and start his doctor day.

He told himself she was in trouble. That she *was* trouble. That she had troubles.

His head got it.

But there was still hot blood zooming up and down his veins. And a stupid smile on his face when he ambled in to greet Rupert Robards.

Rupert had prostate problems. The next patient was an older lady with a lump on her rump, followed by a young mom with a yeast infection and, last for the morning, a sixteen-year-old kid with hot tears in his eyes and a fishing hook stuck deep in his wrist.

There was no room in the entire morning for a single romantic or sexy thought to surface.

Still. She lingered in his mind.

Ginger had parked the Civic right on Magnolia, but once she stormed out of Ike's office, she ignored the car and kept on walking. She needed the exercise. The fresh air. The chance to think.

He'd made her lose her temper twice now.

Usually she could keep her worst flaws under wraps until she'd known a person awhile. Invariably her temper—and other character flaws, such as impulsiveness—couldn't be kept in the closet forever. But somehow Ike had brought out the worst in her right up front.

It would help if he wasn't a doctor. A damn good-looking, sexually appealing doctor. Scruffy. But still adorable.

Steve hadn't been half that adorable, and she'd still been blindsided. Any inkling of attraction for Ike just seemed to work like a trigger for her. Her stay-away button started blinking red and setting off alarm instincts.

She ambled down Magnolia, crossed Oak, aimed down Cypress. It wasn't as if she didn't know the town like the back of her hand. The big stores like Walmart and Target were located in the new section of town, but Sweet Valley's downtown was still vibrant, filled with shop after shop, restaurant after restaurant.

She'd shut down her life in Chicago and zoomed home so fast that she needed some things. Shampoo. Her favorite brand of toothpaste.

En route to the pharmacy, she accidentally spotted a shoe sale.

By the time she'd tried on and bought a pair of sandals, she'd put her mind off handsome, interfering doctors and had her head back where it belonged. On Gramps.

Nothing Ike told her had been reassuring. He'd only opened up more worries, more concerns. She needed to know the truth. She just didn't know what to do about the situation.

Perhaps by instinct, she found herself standing in front of the Butter Bakery. She'd forgotten—or just hadn't had a reason to remember before—that Gramps had an attorney. Ginger knew the name. Louella Meachams. Ginger must have met her sometime—Sweet Valley was such a small town that everyone about met everyone else at some time or another. But Ginger couldn't recall anything about her, until she spotted the sign for Louella Meachams, Esq., just above the stairwell from the bakery.

She couldn't imagine the attorney would be able to see her without an appointment, but she could at least stop by while she was right there in town, set up something.

The old-fashioned stairwell was airless and dark, with steep steps leading to the upstairs offices. Her stomach churned in protest, partly because she'd always been claustrophobic, and partly because she needed to eat something, and soon. She'd planned to have breakfast right after seeing Ike, but that stupid fainting business had stolen her appetite. Still, she'd immediately started to feel better once she'd gotten out in the fresh air. As soon as she made contact with the attorney, she'd stop and get some serious food before heading home.

Upstairs, she found an old-fashioned oak door with the attorney's name on a brass sign. She turned the knob without knocking, assuming she'd be entering a receptionist and lobby area, not the lawyer's specific office.

"Oh. Excuse me. I was hoping to make an appointment with Mrs. Meachams—"

"I'm Louella Meachams. And just Louella would do. Come in. Sit yourself."

The lady had to be around fifty, had a wash-and-wear hairstyle and a general bucket build. She wore men's pants, a starched shirt, no makeup. Hunting dog pictures graced the walls. The sturdy oak chairs facing the desk had no cushions. Windows overlooking the street below had blinds, but no curtains. The whole office looked like a male lawyer's lair, rather than a woman's. And Louella looked a little—maybe even a lot—like a man herself. She peered at her over half-rim glasses.

"I believe you're my grandfather's attorney. Cashner Gautier," Ginger started. "I'm Ginger, his granddaughter. I just got into town a few days ago. And I was hoping you could help me clarify his situation."

"I know who you are, just from all that red hair. You were one fiery little girl. And I'm more than willing to talk with you, but you need to understand that your grandfather's my client. I not only can't, but never would, break confidentiality with him."

"I understand that. And I'd never ask you to." Haltingly she started to explain the situation she'd found at home, how her grandfather wasn't himself, that he seemed to have both memory and health issues, that the place looked in serious disarray compared to the last time she'd been home. Louella leaned back, stuck a leather shoe on a wastebasket for a footrest and listened until she came through with a question.

"As long as I've been Cashner's attorney, I've never been completely clear about his family situation. I know your grandparents only had one child, a daughter—your mother. And that even when your mother married, she kept the Gautier name, which is pretty unusual in these parts. If I have it right, you're now the only close blood kin of Cashner's, because your mama died quite a while ago."

"Yes. Mom was in a terrible car accident. I was barely ten. And that was when I came to live with my grandparents."

"But are there other blood kin? Brothers, cousins? Any relatives at all on your grandfather's side of the fence?"

"No, not that I'm aware of. The Gautiers came originally from France…there may be some distant relatives still there, but none I know of. My grandmother had some family in California, but I never met any of them. They were like second cousins or that distance."

"What about your father?" Louella leaned over, opened a drawer, lifted a sterling silver flask. "Need a little toot?"

"Uh, no. Thank you." She added, "My father

has nothing to do with this situation. He's not a Gautier—"

"Yes. But he's family for you, so he could help you, couldn't he? Advise you on options you might consider for your grandfather."

Ginger frowned. So far she'd given more information than she'd gotten. Not that she minded telling her grandfather's attorney the situation. Gramps trusted Louella. So Ginger did. "My dad," she said carefully, "is about as lovable as you can get. He's huggable, always laughing, lots of fun. I adored him when I was little. He brought me a puppy one birthday, rented a Ferris wheel for another birthday party, took me out of school—played hooky—to fly me to Disney World one year. You'd love him. Everyone does."

"I'm sure there's some reason you're telling me this," Louella said stridently.

"I'm just trying to say, as tactfully as I can, that my dad can't be in this picture. I love him. Not loving him would be like…well, like not loving a puppy. Puppies piddle. It isn't fun to clean up after them, but you can't expect a puppy to behave like a grown-up. Which is to say…I don't even know where my dad is right now. Whatever problems my grandfather has—I'm his person. His problems are mine. And there's nothing I wouldn't do for him."

"All right. I always heard the gossip that your father was your basic good-looking reprobate, but I never met him, didn't know for sure. I'm glad you clarified the situation. I'm sorry that he's out of the picture for you. That makes Cashner's circumstances all the more awkward. But I still can't tell you about his will—"

"I don't give a hoot about his will. I need to know if he's paying his bills. If he's solvent. Can you tell me who has power of attorney? If someone has medical powers? I need to know if I have the right to look into his bank accounts, make sure that bills are being paid, what shape the business is in, whether he's okay financially or if I need to do something."

Louella harrumphed, looked out the window as if she were thinking about how to phrase an answer. Ginger was more than willing to wait.

At least she thought she was. A glance at an old wall clock revealed it was well past noon. Apparently they'd been talking—and she'd been running around town—a lot longer than she'd expected. Technically time didn't matter; it wasn't as if she was on a schedule. But the queasiness that plagued her earlier in the morning was suddenly back. So was exhaustion. Not exhaustion from doing anything; she just had a sudden, consuming urge to curl up in a ball like a cat and close her eyes, just nap for a few minutes.

She'd never been a napper. Until eight weeks ago. Now she could suddenly get so tired she could barely stumble around. It was crazy. She felt crazy. And in a blink of a minute, she just wanted to go home.

"Well, Ginger. I don't know how to say this but bluntly. Your grandfather needs to move out of that big old place. But he won't. He needs to hire someone to take over the tea plantation before it's in complete ruin. But he won't do that, either. And the best advice I can give you is to just leave him alone. Go on about your life. It's what I'd want, if I were in Cashner's situation. He doesn't need or want someone telling him what to do, where he needs to be, what rules he should be following. It won't help. If you want to help, be a good granddaughter and love him. But then just go on with your own life."

Ginger heard her. Alarm shot sparks straight to her bloodstream. Gramps *was* in trouble, in ways the attorney knew about, separate from the problems Ike knew as Gramps's doctor. Urgency made her heart slam. She rushed to her feet—or she tried to.

For the second time that morning, the world turned green and everything in sight started spinning.

"Well, my word!"

She heard Louella's husky voice. Heard it as if it was coming from a hundred yards away. After that, everything went smoky black.

Chapter Three

When the last patient of the morning canceled, Ruby let him know with a fervent "Hallelujah!"

Ike was still smiling when he heard the front door slam—Ruby did like a long lunch when she could get it. But his mind was really on Ginger, and had been all morning.

There was no question that he'd see her again. She'd seek him out because she had to; he was the best source of information on her grandfather. Ike needed that connection just as much, because he happened to love the old man, and something had to be decided about Cashner be-fore the situation turned into a real crisis.

Still, when the office phone rang, he never guessed it would be Ginger contacting him again this soon. Nor would he have thought he'd hear from Louella Meachams—one of his most re-luctant patients. She told him she "had no truck with doctors" every single time he took her blood pressure. Louella was at least part guy. Not gay. Just an exuberantly male kind of female. People trusted her in town. He did, too. She just had a lot of coarse sandpaper in her character.

"Don't waste your time telling me you're busy with a patient, Ike MacKinnon. I don't care if you have fifty patients. I have a woman in my office on the floor. Fainted dead away. Now you get right over here and do something about her."

"Since you asked so nicely, I'll be there right away. But in the meantime…do you know who she is, why she fainted, what happened?"

"I don't care what happened. I want her off

my floor. When she went down, it scared the bejesus out of me. I thought she was dead!"

"I understand—"

"I don't care if you understand or not. You get her out of here somehow, someway, and I'm talking pronto."

"Yes, ma'am. But again…" Hell. Ike just wanted a clue what the problem could be. "Do you know her?"

"Her name is Ginger Gautier. Cashner's grand-daughter. What difference does it make? The problem is I thought she'd stopped breathing. Almost gave me a heart attack. I don't do first aid. I had a sister who fainted all the time, but that was to get our mother's attention. It was fake every time. This is *not* fake. I'm telling you, she went *down.* Right in front of my desk."

"Okay, got it, see you in five, max six."

"You make that three minutes, Doc. And I'm not whistling Dixie."

If Louella really believed there was an emergency, she'd have called 911—but Louella, being stingy, would never risk an ambulance charge unless she was absolutely positive there was no other choice. So Ike took the time to shove on street shoes, grab a jacket and scribble a note to Ruby before heading out.

He could jog the distance faster than driving it—the lawyer's office was only three blocks over, faster yet if he zigzagged through buildings. Pansy let out an unholy howl of abandonment when he left without her, but sometimes, darn it, he just couldn't take his favorite girl.

Less than five minutes later, he reached the bakery and zipped up the steps to the second floor. When he turned the knob of Louella's office, though, something heavy seemed to be blocking it. "Louella, it's me, Doc," he said as he knocked.

Louella opened it. Apparently she'd been the something heavy blocking the entrance. "She keeps trying to leave. Doesn't have a brain cell in her head. I told her she wasn't going anywhere until you checked her out, and that's that."

"I must have said a dozen times that I'm feeling better—and that I was going straight home from here." Ginger's voice was coming from the floor—but it certainly sounded healthy and strong.

"Yeah, I heard you. And I told you a dozen times that there could be liability issues if you left here in shape to cause yourself or others harm."

"You're the only person I've met in a blue moon who's more bullheaded than I am, bless your heart. But keeping a person against their will is called kidnapping. Or is there another legal term?"

While the two women continued this pleasant conversation, Ike hunkered down—apparently Louella had threatened Ginger with death if she tried to get up before the doctor got there. He went through the routine. Pulse. Temp. Whether she could focus, whether she had swollen lymph glands.

Wherever he touched her, she jumped.

He liked that. If he was stuck feeling walloped this close to her, he at least wanted her to suffer the same way.

He got some extra personal contact—judicious, but lucky for sure—when he helped her to her feet. She didn't wobble. Of course, with his arm around her, she couldn't have wobbled—or fallen—even if she'd wanted to. But she shot him one of those ice-blue looks to indicate he could remove his hands. Now. Right now.

"Okay, Louella, I'm taking her from your office."

"And don't let her come back here until she's fit as a fiddle."

"My. I had no idea that fiddles had health issues. Like whether they could be fit or sick. I had no idea they were alive at all—"

Ike saw the look on Louella's face, could see

she was in a rolling up the sleeves to get into another squabble, so he shuffled Ginger quickly into the hall.

He saw her sudden choke when they reached the top of her stairs, so he suspected she was still a little on the dizzy side. He hooked an arm around her, making sure she was steady.

"You don't need to do that," she said irritably.

"Can't have you falling on my watch."

"I'm not on your watch."

"Uh-huh. You know…you *could* have been nice to Louella."

"She wasn't nice to me first!"

"You seriously scared her when you fainted."

"That's an excuse for holding me hostage and not letting me leave? For insulting me? For calling you?"

"Yup. At least, that's how I see it. But then, I don't have your temper."

At the bottom of the stairs, he'd barely pushed

open the door before she shot through. She took a step west before he kidnapped her wrist.

"Hey. My car is that way—"

"And you'll be in your car in about a half hour. But first, you need an immediate medical intervention."

"Intervention? What are you talking about?"

The New York Deli was at the corner of Magnolia. Whether anything served had anything to do with New York, no one knew or cared. The place was always packed at lunch, but Feinstein—the owner—always saved a table for Ike. It was bribery, pure and simple. Feinstein was worried about the performance of his boy parts. He'd never had any marital problems with his wife before, but "everybody" knew guys eventually needed a little chemical boost. Which was to say, Feinstein had motivation for taking good care of the town doctor.

Ike never came for the bribe. He came for the food. And Ginger continued to make minor protestations about being herded like a sheep, but that was only until she saw the menu.

Mrs. Feinstein—possibly the homeliest woman Ike had ever seen—advised Ginger on the best choices, and who could have guessed? Ginger agreed without arguing.

Right off, she devoured three pickles. Then a masterful corned beef on rye. Chips. Cole slaw. Since she picked at the crumbs after that, he figured she was still hungry, so he ordered dessert. Apple cake with whipped cream.

Then more pickles.

He leveled a sandwich, too, which took all of a minute and a half. So while her mouth was full, he took the opportunity to start a conversation. "I'm guessing that before the evening news, the whole town will know that you fainted twice this morning, that we're having lunch together…and they'll likely be speculating on whether we're sleeping together."

She dropped her fork, which he took as encouraging. So he went on, "My theory is…we might as well sleep together, since we've already been branded with the tag."

She dropped her fork—again—but then she just squinted her eyes at him. He didn't see temper this time, just reluctant humor. "Hey. Do you usually flirt with women you think are pregnant by someone else?"

"Not usually, no. In fact, never." He retrieved a couple fresh forks from the table next to them, then went back for another couple. Who knew how many she would need before this meal was over. "But I keep finding your situation, well, unique. You came home because you were really worked up about your grandfather. But there's no guy here. If you had a guy, he'd have to be a class-A jerk not to be with you when he knows you need help."

"Wow. That analysis and conclusion is just stunning."

"Yeah, my mama always said I was a bright

boy," he agreed with his best deadpan expression. "So my theory is…there's no guy to stop me from moving in on you."

This time she had to chuckle—clearly in spite of herself. "I've been doing a lot of hurling and fainting. Most guys would run in the opposite direction."

"Most guys haven't been through medical school."

"That's an answer?"

"What can I say? A first-year resident loses any chance of being embarrassed ever again in his life. Some things just come with life. Now what's that expression about?"

She lifted a hand. "I was just thinking. I had this sudden instinct…that you just might be a hardcore, card-carrying good guy." She put a stop sign into another hand gesture. "I'm not accusing you of anything terrible. I just didn't expect to even let a positive thought anywhere near you. So I'm just saying. If I was ever going to trust a doctor again as long as I live—which I'm not—it might have been you."

"Ah. It's the doctor thing that's a problem. You're such a relief."

"Relief?"

"Practically every single woman in this town has been feeding me, taking care of me, fluttering her eyelashes at me. All their mamas think of doctors as being a terrific catch. You know, dumb as a fish that just needs the right bait to sucker in. You're so much more fun. I'd ask you out…but I'm afraid if we had a good time, you'd quit disliking me, and then where would we be? Not having fun together anymore. It's not worth the risk. Still, I don't see why we shouldn't sleep together. That doesn't have to interfere with your giving me a constant hard time. We could just redirect all that passionate energy a little differently when the lights go off."

She cupped her chin. "Did anything you just said make a lick of sense?"

He didn't care if he was making sense. She'd had a rotten morning—a stressful visit with him, then a stressful visit with the lawyer, no easy answers about her grandfather. And he hadn't known until he'd sneaked the information that the father of her baby was both a doctor and a louse.

She was flying solo. Flying solo with a pregnancy and no help in sight.

But he'd gotten her fed. And teased. And almost laughing. She'd forgotten it all for a while.

Sometimes that was the best a doctor could do. Offer some stress relief. There was no way any doctor could cure all ills…much less all wrongs.

When she glanced at a wall clock, he did, too. He was startled at how much time had passed. Ruby was going to kill him. He was ten minutes late for his first afternoon patient.

"Yeah, I didn't realize how late it was, either. I need to get back to my grandfather."

He put some money down, knowing the Feinsteins wouldn't give him a check, and eventually steered her to the door. There was the usual gauntlet of "Hi, Doc!" and "Ginger, so glad to hear you're back in town" and other ferocious attempts to stall them. He kept moving them as fast as he could.

Outside, the sky was pumping out clouds now. A whiskery wind tossed paper and litter in the air, lifted collars. The temperature was still warmish, somewhere in the sixties, but there was rain in the wind, and the bright sun kept hiding from sight.

"I see your car," he said.

"You don't have to walk me there. You have to be in a hurry to get back to your office."

"It all comes with the service. A lady faints, she gets walked to her car."

"What if she isn't a lady?"

"If a wicked woman faints, she still gets walked to her car. It's in the rule book."

"What rule book is that?"

"The *South Carolina Rules for Gentlemen* rule book. My mom made me memorize whole passages before I was four. She called it getting ready for kindergarten." Walking next to her felt like foreplay. It was kind of a test of rhythms.

Whether they could walk together, move together in a natural way. How his height worked with hers. Whether she could keep up with his stride. Whether she wanted to. Whether she galloped on ahead when he wanted to amble.

Fast, too damned fast, they reached her rust bucket of a Civic. She dipped in her shoulder bag for her car key, found it, lifted her head and suddenly frowned at him.

"What?" He had no idea what her expression meant. Even less of an idea what she planned to do.

She popped up on tiptoe, framed his face between her soft palms and kissed him. On a guy's scale of kisses, it was only a two. No tongue. No pressure. No invitation.

More…just a short, evocative melding of textures. Her lips. His lips.

Like a meeting of whipped cream and chocolate.

Or like brandy and a winter fire.

Or like the snug of gloves on a freezing morning.

Or like that click, that electric high-charge surge, not like the million kisses you've had since middle school, not like the any-girl-would-do kisses, but the click kind. The wonder kind. The damn it, what the hell is happening here kind.

She pulled back, sank back, cocked her head and looked at him. Her purse fell.

He picked it up. Her keys fell. He picked those up, too.

When he got his breath back, he said carefully, "Do we have any idea why you did that?"

"I've been known to do some very bad, impulsive things sometimes. Even if I regret it. Even if I know I'm going to regret it later."

"So that was just a bad impulse." He shook his head. "Sure came across like a great impulse to me." Before she could try selling him any more malarkey, he said, "I stop to see your grandfather at least twice a week. Always short visits. He pretends it's not about his health. So do I. Which is to say…I'll see you soon. Very soon. And that's a promise."

But not soon enough. His heart slammed.

Of course, that was the man talking, and not the doctor. Sometimes it was okay to be both roles…but not with her, he sensed. Never with her.

Ginger had barely pulled in the drive when the rain started. It was just a spatter when she stepped out, but the sky cracked with a streak of lightning by the time she reached the porch.

Thunder growled. Clouds started swirling as

if a child had finger-painted the whole sky with grays. Pretty, but ominous. Inside, she called, "Gramps? I'm home!" The dark had infiltrated the downstairs with gloom, somehow accenting the dust and neglect that seemed everywhere. Still, she heard voices—and laughter—coming from the kitchen.

At the kitchen doorway, she folded her arms, having to smile at the two cronies at the kitchen table. The game looked to be cutthroat canasta. Money was on the table. Cards all over the place. From the time she'd left that morning, a set of dirty china seemed to have accumulated on the sink counter, but the two old codgers were having a blast.

She bent down to kiss her grandfather. Got a huge hug back. And for now, his eyes were lucid and dancing-clear. "You've been gone all day, you little hussy. Hope you spent a lot of money shopping and had a great old time."

"I did." The two rounds of fainting and encounters with Ike were locked up in her mind's closet. Her grandfather recognized her. Had a happy, loving smile for her. "Cornelius, you're getting a hug from me, too, so don't try running."

Cornelius pretended he was trying to duck under the table, but that was all tease. He took his hug like a man. Cornelius was smaller than she was, and possibly had some Asian and black and maybe Native American blood. For certain no one else looked quite like him. Ginger had never known whether her family had adopted him or the other way around, but he and Gramps were of an age. Neither could manage to put a glass in the dishwasher. Neither obeyed an order from anyone. And both of them could while away a dark afternoon playing cards and having a great time.

"All right, you two. I'm going upstairs for a short nap."

"Go. Go." She was promptly shooed away, as

Cornelius chortled over some card played and both men issued raucous, enthusiastically gruesome death threats to each other.

Apparently the morning had been tough on her system, because once her head hit the pillow upstairs, she crashed harder than a whipped puppy. She woke up to a washed-clean world and the hour was past four. After a fast shower, she flew downstairs to find her boys on the front veranda now, rocking and sipping sweet tea and arguing about a ball game.

When Cornelius saw her, he pushed out of the rocker. "We was thinking you might not wake up until tomorrow, you were looking so tired."

"I was a little tired, but I'm feeling great now."

Cornelius nodded. "I'm headed to the kitchen. Got some supper cooking. Can't remember what all I started right now, but should be ready in an hour or so."

"That'd be great, you." She planned to head into the kitchen and help him—but not yet. Her gramps's eyes were still clear, still bright. She pulled a rocker closer to him, sat down.

"Gramps. All these years, you had Amos Hawthorne managing the land, running the farm. But no one's mentioned him, and I haven't seen him around."

"That's because he's not here anymore. I had to fire him. I don't remember exactly when it happened. But he stopped doing what I told him. He badgered and badgered me, until I said I'd had enough. Let him go."

Ginger gulped. "So…who's handling the tea now? The shop? The grounds?"

"Well, I am, honey child. Me and Cornelius. We closed the shop after…" He frowned. "I don't know exactly when. A little while ago."

"Okay. So who's doing the grounds around the house? The mowing. The gardens and trees and all."

"Cornelius and I had a theory about that. We need some goats."

"Goats," Ginger echoed.

"Yup. We have a heap of acreage that's nothing but lawn. Goats love grass. Wouldn't cost us a thing. The goats could eat the grass without using a lick of gas or needing a tractor at all."

Ginger was getting a thump of anxiety in her tummy again. "So…right now we don't have a lawn service or a farm manager?"

"We both think goats could do the work. They'd be happy. We'd be happy. Don't you think that sounds like fun, sweetheart?"

"I do. I do." She'd inherited the ability to lie from her father. "Gramps, do you know who did your taxes last year? I mean, do you have an accountant in town?"

"Why, honey, you know your grandma does all that. I always oversaw the business, the farm. But it was your grandma who did all the work with figures. We never depended on outsiders for that kind of thing. Why are you asking all these questions? We can do something fun. Like play cards. Or put out the backgammon board. After dinner, we could take the golf cart around before the bugs hit."

He was right, Ginger realized. There was no point in asking any more questions. Every answer she'd heard so far was downright scary. There appeared to be no one running the place. Not the tea plantation. Not the house. Gramps seemed under the impression that Grandma was still alive, still there with him. The whole situation was more overwhelming than she'd ever expected.

Ginger wondered if she could somehow will herself to faint again. It certainly helped her block out things earlier that day…. Except that fainting brought on Ike, as if he had some invisible radar when anything embarrassing or upsetting was happening to her.

She still couldn't figure out what possessed her to kiss him. He'd been a white knight, sort of. And she'd been starving and hadn't realized it. And a simple gesture like a hug or a kiss just didn't seem like that big a deal....

But it was.

It was a big deal because she already knew she was susceptible to doctors.

She also knew that impulsiveness got her into trouble every time. A woman could make a mistake. Everyone did that. No one could avoid it. But the measure of a woman was partly how she handled those mistakes.

Fool me once, shame on you. Fool me twice, shame on me. She'd been trying to drill that mantra into her head. A doctor might seem like great husband potential for lots of women—but not her. Doctors invariably put their jobs first, their own needs, and played by their own rule book.

Ike for sure played by his own rule book.

Keeping her heart a long, long way away from him was an easy for-sure.

Chapter Four

The next day, by midmorning, Ginger was not only reenergized, but conquering the world at the speed of sound. She'd put both boys to work by wrapping microfiber fabric around their shoes. Their job was to shuffle around the entire downstairs. It might not be the most glamorous way to dust the hardwood floors, but it was good enough. They were, of course, complaining mightily.

She'd hunkered down in the kitchen to clean, and figured she wasn't likely to escape the room for another three years at best. She'd found flour moths. That discovery canceled out any other plans she'd had for the day. She immediately started removing everything from the cupboards. Her first thought was to wash every surface with bleach, but she worried fumes that strong couldn't be good with a pregnancy, so she pulled on old plastic gloves, mixed up strong soap and a disinfectant, then unearthed a serious scrub brush.

The top west side cupboards were completely emptied out when she was interrupted by the sound of a motor—a lawn motor. She glanced outside, and then immediately climbed down and sprinted outside. A total stranger was driving a green lawn-mowing tractor. She'd never seen either the tractor or the man before, but once she chased after him—and finally won his attention—she could at least make out his features. He was an older black man, with a graying head of hair and soft eyes.

He shut off the mower when he spotted her.

"I don't understand," she started with. "Who are you and why are you here?"

"I'm Jed, ma'am."

His voice was liquid sweet, but that explained precisely nothing. "You don't work for my grandfather."

"No, ma'am. I'm retired. Don't work no more."

When she started another question, he gently interrupted with a more thorough explanation. "I stopped working anything regular, but I'm sure not ready for a rocking chair yet, and I have time on my hands. Dr. Ike now, he delivered my grandchild, knowing ahead the family couldn't pay him. So I'm paying it off this way. By doing things he finds for me to do. Not to worry. I'll check the oil and the gas and the blades when I put the mower back in the shop. I know my way around tractors."

She didn't know what to say, and when she didn't come up with anything fast enough, he just tipped his baseball cap and started the noisy motor again.

She stood there, hands on hips, and debated whether to call Ike immediately to give him what for...or to wait. Waiting seemed the wiser choice, because he'd be in the middle of his workday, likely seeing patients. So she went back toward the kitchen, thinking that the cleaning chore would give her time to think up what to say to him, besides.

She checked on Gramps and Cornelius, who'd turned on a radio to some station channeling rock and roll from the 1950s. But they were moving—at least until she showed up, and then they complained that they were too old to do this much exercise, that she was killing them, that she was cruel. She brewed everyone a fresh pot of Charleston's Best—everybody's favorite tea—then sent them back to work.

The kitchen looked as insurmountable as it had when she left it—but it wasn't as if she had an option to give up. The job had to be done, so she hunkered back down. She had her head under the sink when she heard the front doorbell.

She waited, thinking that her guys would obviously answer it—but no. The bell rang. Then rang again. She stood up and yanked off her plastic gloves as she stomped down the hall. A lady was on the other side of the screen door. A plump lady, wearing an old calico dress, her thin brown hair tied up in a haphazard bun.

"I know who you are," she said gruffly. "You're Cashner's granddaughter, Ginger Gautier. And I'm your new cook."

Ginger frowned. "I don't understand. We don't have a cook."

"Well, you do now. I don't do tofu, I'm telling you right off. No sushi, either. You want something fancy, you need somebody else."

Ginger started to speak, but the woman was downright belligerent, particularly for someone who'd shown up out of the blue. Without giving her any chance to answer, the lady pushed open the screen door and marched herself inside, aiming straight down the hall to the kitchen.

"Now just wait one minute. I don't even know who you are."

"My name's Sarah. Just Sarah. And like I said, I already know you're Ginger. Your grandma and I used to help out at church dinners now and then. A great lady, your grandma. Knew the value of a day's work, she did. Good grief."

When Sarah-Just-Sarah reached the doorway to the kitchen, she whipped around with an annoyed expression. "This kitchen is a complete mess. No one could cook in there right now."

Ginger threw up her hands. "I'd have told you that. If it was any of your business. Or if you'd asked."

Sarah ignored her, just propped her hands on her hips as she poked and peered around at the kitchen set up. "Well, here's the thing. The court says I got a problem with anger management. I don't think so. I think you'd be mad, too, if you had a no-count bum of a husband like mine. So the thing is, I got three children to feed. Which means I can't take on jobs where you have to show up for regular hours. My youngest one is on the sickly side, besides. So I'll just show up as I can. I'll get a meal cooking or a slow cooker going or whatever's going to work that day. You'll be able to eat it hot or just reheat. I'm a good cook. Close to a great cook. No one's ever complained about my cooking. Ever."

"I'm sure that's true. If I was looking for a cook. But—"

Sarah-Just-Sarah's chin shot up another notch. "Dr. Ike. He's been seeing my kids since he came to town. That's almost four years. I paid him when I could, but I could never seem to hold a job, between the kids and my no-good husband. So I'd bring Dr. Ike cookies or a pie, or maybe cornbread with wildflower honey. Anyways, when all three of my kids got sick in September, he didn't even send me a bill. Never even brought it up. And the thing was, I couldn't even try to work then, not with sick kids. So I cornered him, I did. Said I was nobody's charity case, even if I couldn't immediately pay my bill. And he said, 'I could need a favor down the pike.' So I'm his favor. Well, holy moly. You are in a mess in here, aren't you?"

Every word that came out of the woman's mouth sounded angry. Ginger hadn't been able to get a word in, but she was starting to get the picture that Sarah simply talked that way. Mad. And even more mad as she squinted at the scandalized war zone in the kitchen.

It wasn't as if Ginger could help it. She was in the worst part of the mess, of course. Drawers gaped open, drying from where she'd washed inside. Water had sloshed on the floor here and there. Buckets blocked anyone from walking around. Cans from some of the lower cabinets were strewn on the ground while those shelves got cleaned. The dishwasher was running. The table was covered with rolls of shelf paper, which Ginger expected to cover the surfaces—once the place had been disinfected and cleaned and dried.

"There is no possibility I could cook in this mess," Sarah said stridently.

"Well, of course you can't," Ginger said crossly.

"But then, neither could you. So this afternoon, I'll just drop off dinner. Say around six. And at that time, I'll fill out a little schedule for you, so you know what food I'm making and when I'm making it. You'll need to grocery shop. I'm not doing that."

Ginger lifted her fingertips to her temple. She had the oddest headache. "Of course you wouldn't shop for me—"

"But I'll give you a list of what to buy. For the dinners. Whatever you want to eat for breakfast or lunch, that's on you, not me."

"Now you just wait a minute—"

But Sarah ignored her again, said something rude and dismissive, and then just marched for the front door as furiously fast as she'd walked in.

Ginger stared after her, aghast. One crazy encounter that morning had been bewildering enough—but two? In the same day? People didn't behave like that. Not normal people.

It was as if some unseen force had instructed both Jed and Sarah to ignore any attempt she made to say no.

That unseen-force was a three-letter word, of course. *Ike.* But that was precisely the upsetting part. She was in over her head in every way, and was likely to be overwhelmed by messes and problems for a good long time. For just those reasons, she wanted no association with Ike. She didn't want to be thinking about kissing and that look in his eyes and her making an idiot of herself every time she was near him.

She didn't want to think about Ike.

She half turned and faced her wreck of a kitchen again. She didn't have time for a heart attack or a mental breakdown. Maybe later in the day, but not now.

She searched out her guys, found they'd tried hiding in rockers on the veranda. That was okay, they'd done more than enough work for the day. She made sandwiches, took them out on a tray, and by the time they'd finished a makeshift lunch, the boys were nodding off. She headed back to the kitchen.

The war zone finally started to turn the corner. In another hour, all surfaces were scrubbed and sparkling. Cupboards were all lined with fresh paper. She'd saved the worst for last—the very top cupboard shelves to the right of the sink. It was like the mystery shelf in every house—the place that no one could reach—and was inevitably filled with things no one had seen in decades. Dishes with cracks. Dishes that had no function anyone could think of. Teapots—the ugly ones that Grandma had never wanted in the living room collection. Dust. Peppermint schnapps. Tequila—five bottles, all with the worms.

She didn't want to do it. Her back ached. Her fingers and hands felt sore from scrubbing. Her shoulders and arms were whining about how she'd abused them for hours now.

But there was just that one last shelf. And then she'd be completely done.

She crawled up and then stood up on the counter, scrub brush in hand—which was when she heard a rap on the door—for the third interruption that day.

This time, though, she was ready. She climbed down and bolted for the front door. Unfortunately, Gramps and Cornelius were still out on the front veranda. Before she could push open the screen, she could hear her guys and their joyful greetings for the visitor.

She could have raced to the bathroom to

freshen up, but what was the point? He'd already seen her at her worst. Twice. And it wasn't as if she was trying to attract the man. So she was wearing plastic gloves and no shoes and her hair hadn't seen a brush in a *long* time, not counting the lack of makeup or the details.

And of course, it was Ike. Ike and the slobbering, mournful hound, who dragged herself up the steps only to fall in a heap in everyone's way.

Pansy only looked half as disreputable as her owner. Ike wore a clay-colored T-shirt that was frayed at the neck, a derelict pair of shorts, sandals that looked to be about a hundred years old. Maybe he'd shaved yesterday.

Still, she felt it. The fever climbing up from her toes, weakening her heart. There were fevers and there were fevers. A fever of ninety-nine, anyone started to feel yucky. A fever of one hundred generally brought her to her knees. A fever of one-oh-one and she knew she was in deep trouble, sick trouble. Only when a fever reached around a hundred and two did some weird factor kick in, and she started to feel euphoric. Goofy euphoric. High and giddy and crazy. All fear gone. All reality dismissed from sight.

That was precisely how she felt around Ike. The wrong kind of fever.

And he was looking at her the same way. The wrong kind of way.

Gramps and Cornelius were still asking why he'd come by.

"Well, I sure didn't come to see you two old reprobates," he said wryly. "I came to see Ginger. Because I figured around now she was planning to tear a strip off my hide, and I might as well get it over with."

"Why on earth?" Cornelius asked.

"Yeah, why on earth," Ginger echoed.

"I suspect you think I should have asked you first, before sending out some help."

"You could have asked me. But then, I needed help. Which you knew."

She saw the slightest frown crease his forehead. Probably he wasn't expecting her calm, amiable tone—not just because of the circumstances, but because he'd never heard it before. "I did know you could use a hand," he agreed. "I also had patients who needed to pay their own way. So it seemed like a good idea to me. Nobody gets hurt. Everyone gets something they need."

"Except," she said gently, "that it was manipulative and domineering. You didn't ask first. You just assumed you knew best. What was best for me. What was best for my grandfather. I asked around, but I couldn't find anyone who elected you God."

"Ouch," Ike said.

She didn't respond, just headed back in the house. She didn't lock the screen door, just gave it the opportunity to close with a decided *thwack.*

Ike winced when the door slammed, then scratched the back of his neck.

"What on earth did you do to that girl to set her off?" Cornelius demanded.

Cashner set his chair rocking again. "She's a firecracker. Always has been. Always will be. If I were you, Doc, I'd steer clear for a while."

Cornelius looked at him. "Don't listen to him. Listen to me. If you let her fester on her own, she'll build up a heap of temper. Then you'll leave and we'll be left here to get the brunt of it."

"Well, I guess that's true," Cashner reluctantly admitted. "Ike, you best go after her. Believe it. We'll both stay out here, out of your way completely."

Cashner was lucid for a change—a good sign. Cornelius was even making sense. So Ike could put those two concerns out of his mind, at least for a few minutes. "Pansy, stay," he murmured, and then aimed inside.

He found Ginger by following the fumes.

She was standing on the kitchen counter in her bare feet. Her goal was apparently to empty the contents from the top cupboard shelf. Two bottles of tequila were open and in the process of pouring down the drain, and she was about to lean down with a third. When she saw him in the doorway, she jumped.

He surged forward at rocket speed, scared she'd fall—a risk that was hardly far-fetched, considering her behavior the other day. Yet when he sprinted close enough to lift his arms to support her, she moved back an inch. Just enough so he didn't touch her. And said crossly, "I wasn't going to fall. You just startled me."

"You startled me, too. Or the smell did. I take it you don't like tequila?"

"I have no idea. But you can take it to the bank, I won't be drinking anything with worms in the bottle. Years ago, Gramps had an employee, worked in the tea, always brought Gramps a bottle at the end of the season. They kept accumulating. Grandma and I just ignored them. She had the same feeling about the worms that I did." Then, "If you came for another kiss, you're not going to get one."

"What makes you think I want to kiss you? You've got a smudge on your cheek. Your knees are all red. Your hair is as wild as a rusty Brillo pad."

"You came for another kiss," she informed him. "Beats me why. I'm a wreck. It's obvious. You can't possibly believe this could go anywhere."

He didn't. At least not exactly. The problem was more confounding than that. He'd been content with his laid-back lifestyle in Sweet Valley for all this time—or so he'd believed until he ran into her. Crazy or not, he felt more invigorated after tussling with her for two minutes than in the whole four years before her. "I'm not admitting anything—except that I might have come back for another kiss. But I also came to find out how much trouble I was in for sending over Jed and Sarah."

"Well, that's a different subject. I'm not sure Jed took to me, but I sure took to him. He knows the front from the back end of a tractor. I sure don't." She crouched down, but instead of jumping to the floor, she just sat on the sink counter. She reached for the last two tequila bottles, opened both and then turned them upside down to pour in the sink. "Now Sarah—I'm not so sure. She sure has an ornery side."

"Well, yeah. But that's why I thought you two might get along. You're two peas in a pod and all that."

She squinted at him. "Are you suggesting that I'm ornery?"

"I would never do that," he assured her. "Stubborn, yes. Temper prone, yes. A spark plug ready to fire, yes. A volcano always ready to erupt at the slightest provoca—"

There. A smile. So reluctant. But the darned woman couldn't just throw out a good sense of humor, even when she was trying her best to stay crabby.

"*Only* because I'm a Southern girl raised with manners, I'll offer you something to drink. Something short and quick."

"What have you got? Besides all that tequila."

"Was that a real question?" She rolled her eyes. "This was a tea plantation. Tea's the only drink we serve morning, noon and night."

"Well, I guess I wouldn't mind a cup of… hmm…tea."

She finally hopped down from the counter, gave him a single poke in the stomach. "You're not as funny as you think you are."

"You're still smiling."

"That may be because I'm a lunatic." Some habits were clearly ingrained in her, without her having to think twice. Making tea was a ritual in her grandparents' house. The right pot. The right temperature water. The decision about which tea. The smelling of the leaves, the measuring. And finally the wait, while the tea steeped.

Ike had watched her grandfather do it a dozen times. Even where Cashner's other memories were fading fast, he knew how to make good tea like he knew how to wake up in the morning.

So did she.

"Don't ask for cream or sugar. They're both sins in this house. For the right tea, you shouldn't need any extras."

"I figured that out the first time your grandfather served me tea. He almost took my head off when I asked for some sweetener. Got a three-hour lecture on tea. I never made that mistake again."

"I'll be darned. A man who learns. Who knew there was such a thing?"

He winced, watching her pull out cups that matched the teapot. "Speaking of men in your life," he said casually, "Does he know? About the pregnancy?"

"And here I thought we were going to have a nice conversation." She handed him his cup.

"So. You haven't told him. But you must have an idea how he's likely to respond when he finds out you're pregnant."

She poured a cup for herself, but now she immediately set it down. "That's it. Out. Out, out, out. I wouldn't have minded talking to you a little more about my gramps. But not now. Another time. When I'm not so likely to brain you with the nearest hard, sharp object."

"Okay," he agreed. "We don't need any more conversation."

As quickly as he put down his tea, he reached for her. She wasn't expecting it. Being pulled into his arms. Having a kiss laid on her mouth the way a bee zoned on pollen.

He hadn't expected to kiss her, either. It hadn't even been on his mind—until she brought it up—and then he couldn't think about anything but getting his hands on her. Talk about lunacy.

She'd been nothing but testy and difficult. She was pregnant by someone else. She had a heap of trouble, and who knew if she'd even stay in this little Southern burg for any longer than she had to. But that was his practical side talking.

Right now the only communication going on was between his mouth and hers. Especially hers. The taste of her, the smell of her skin, the sweetness of her lips put a buzz in his blood that refused to shut off. He was a laid-back guy, by choice. He wanted a small life, not a big one. He wanted time to care, to play, to share, and if that meant a sacrifice in money and possessions, so be it.

But this kiss—her sweet, sweet taste—was stressful on a par with a tsunami. It was all her doing…because she tasted like no other woman tasted. Because she gripped his shoulders and hung on. Because she acted volatile, dizzy, weak, as if he was the sexiest connection she'd ever made, even if it was only for a kiss.…

Even if that only a kiss barely, sparely involved the tease of her soft, warm breasts, the look of her eyelashes sweeping her cheeks, the way her slim hands clenched on his shoulders, the way she made a groan. Or a moan. A sound as if she didn't mind this insane rocket ride.

Damn it. It was just a kiss.

Except that he didn't end it. Couldn't end it.

Until she suddenly bolted back, her eyes snapping open, looking dazed and confused. "Ike. I keep hearing drums."

"Me, too."

"I mean...I think I'm really hearing drums."

"Oh. Afraid that's my cell phone."

"Your cell phone. Plays a drumroll." That dazed look was disappearing awfully fast. She'd liked those kisses. As much as he had. But now she seemed to be recalling that he wasn't her favorite person on the planet.

"Yes. And unfortunately, I'm afraid it's Tildey."

"And Tildey is...?"

"Tildey's twenty-nine. Two weeks overdue with her third baby. This time, she got a midwife. Didn't want to pay for a doc and a hospital."

"There has to be a 'but' in there," Ginger said. They'd both moved back. There were inches between them...except where his arms were still wrapped around her. She divested them, one at a time. His right arm dropped heavily at his side. Ditto for his left arm. Both arms seemed to have lost all muscle strength.

"But Tildey never really trusted the midwife from the get-go. She's been calling three times a week for some backup information. And she called this morning, to let me know she was in labor. And that the midwife was already there."

"I'll bet this conversation makes sense to one of us," Ginger said dryly.

"I'm guessing she's around five centimeters by now. And in a fair panic."

"Then you'd better go."

"I need to," he agreed, but truthfully, he still felt shell-shocked. Or Ginger-shocked. How the woman could pack so much zesty, earthy, compelling sexiness into a few kisses…well. She was downright dangerous.

But of course, he had to pull himself back together. And he would. He always did. "Whether you believe it or not, I came by because I thought you might need to talk more about your grandfather."

She hesitated. "I do."

"All right. Next time. We'll do a serious talk. Honest." When his cell did a second, fresh drumroll, he said swiftly, "Would you mind if Pansy stayed here? Just for a little while. Normally I either leave her home or bring her with me. But I don't want to take the time to drive home, and this isn't a household where I can take her—"

"Ike. I don't know dogs. And I definitely don't know bloodhounds. I have no idea what—"

"Thanks. Really. And I promise I'll be back as quickly as I can."

That was the plan. To check on Tildey, make sure the delivery was going okay with the midwife and then leave.

Unfortunately, the midwife turned out to have the brain of a flea, Tildey was in trouble and so was the baby. Her two other kids were wandering around, crying and scared, and definitely too young to be left alone. Tildey's husband had apparently left for the bar when she first went into labor and no one had seen him since.

By the time Ike could finally drive back to the Gautiers', the hour was well past midnight. The bright day had turned upside down; the sky was belching clouds and hurtling lightning and having a noisy, stormy tantrum. Rain attacked him the instant he climbed out of his truck. He raced to the front door—not expecting anyone to be awake, or intending to awaken anyone this late. He just had to pick up Pansy, who he'd assumed would be waiting for him on the porch.

She wasn't. She was nowhere to be seen.

Ike stepped back, looked up and around. As far as he could tell, there was only one light on in the entire house. On the second story, in the far east window, he caught sight of the soft yellow glow of lamplight.

Chapter Five

Dinner was a feast. Ginger never saw or heard Sarah in the house; she just found the lavish feast when she popped in the kitchen after five. The casserole dish had instructions taped to the tinfoil. Chicken in some kind of fabulous cheese sauce filled a big pan, with broiled baby potatoes in another. A loaf of French bread—fresh-baked, still warm—sat on the counter, along with instructions not to overcook the butter beans.

Gramps ate as if it was his last meal.

Cornelius, who rarely stayed for dinner, kept heaping on more helpings.

There were only a couple of problems. One was that Gramps kept calling her Rachel. And the other was the dog.

"Sweetheart, I can't believe you let the dog inside. You've never liked dogs inside," Gramps said.

"I didn't let her inside. She howled at the top of her lungs when Ike left. There was nothing else I could do." That wasn't the only problem with the dog, of course. Ginger wasn't certain how much the bloodhound weighed, but at the moment a hundred pounds—at *least*—of dead weight stuck closer to her leg than glue.

Apparently the hound felt insecure when Ike wasn't there.

Cornelius kept feeding the dog tidbits of chicken. Gramps had been steadily feeding her butter beans. The hound would eat any and everything, but immediately came back to lean against Ginger.

She also drooled.

Ginger had filled a bowl of water—which the dog had gulped down and she'd had to refill three times now. They'd fed her from dinner because they didn't have regular dog food and didn't know when Ike would be back. It had to be soon, though, Ginger thought. Obviously babies arrived in their own chosen time—but there was a midwife there, he'd said. So he had to be back soon.

She told herself that every time she glanced at a clock. It only took a few minutes to pile dishes in the dishwasher, even with Pansy glued to her side. Cornelius finally took off for his quarters—the small house on the other side of the garage. Gramps lingered a little longer.

"We could sit on the porch for a spell, Rachel."

She started to correct him, then stopped. It didn't seem to help, and when push came down to shove, she didn't really care if he called her Rachel or Loretta or any other darned name he wanted to. "It's turned too cold, Gramps. Temperature's been dropping like a stone, and it smells like the wind's bringing on a storm."

"Will you come in and watch TV with me, then? Our favorite show is on at nine."

"I will, Gramps. Give me a hug."

He stretched out his arms, and snuggled against her for a big, warm hug.

"I love you," she said.

"And I love you right back, sweetheart. What do you say we call Ginger tonight? I really miss her."

Ginger sucked in a breath. Every time she thought she'd accepted the changes in Gramps, something else happened. It hurt, that he could be talking right to her and still not know who she was.

The next couple hours were just as unsettling. She finished the kitchen chores, let Pansy out, let Pansy in, brewed a cup of oolong for Gramps and then asked if he wanted to play a game of backgammon.

"You're ready to lose, are you, honey?"

He loved the game, she knew. When she was a girl, they'd played almost every night after dinner. And he perked up, starting chuckling and teasing, having a good time. It took her a few minutes to realize that he was moving pieces that made no sense. He thought he was playing the game, but he didn't seem to have a clue what he was doing.

By the time he went to bed, Ginger felt shaken. Her grandfather seemed to lose more ground every day. Unsettled and uneasy, she ambled around the house. She found Ike's cell phone in the kitchen—which provoked a sharp, strong memory of his kissing her just hours before. The point, though, was that he could likely have borrowed someone else's phone to call if he thought he was going to be much longer.

She wandered to the front doors, peering out. The evening had turned pitch-black, devil black. Clouds tumbled over each other, racing in fast from the west. The rain had started, not a downpour yet, but it looked like the battalion of clouds beyond had the heaviest artillery.

Her sidekick nuzzled her leg. "Yeah, you want Ike back, too, don't you?" She bent down to rub Pansy's ears. "We need a plan here. You want to sleep on the porch? Or just inside? I promise. He'll be here." Ginger crossed her fingers. She was pretty sure Ike would never leave his dog. "You could lie in front of the door, like you did before. Then you'll see him when he drives in. Doesn't that sound like a good plan?"

Pansy seemed okay with the idea, was coaxed outside, ambled down the steps to pee and then heaved back up the steps and collapsed.

Ginger headed upstairs for the bathtub, and was just sinking into the warm soothing water when a low rumble of thunder boomed from the west. Instantly, Pansy let out a howl that could have wakened the dead. Ginger peeled out of the tub, grabbed a towel, ran downstairs and let the dog in.

"We are not going to do that again. I get it. You don't like storms. No problem. You can sleep inside. But no more howling!"

Ginger closed the big doors but left them unlocked for Ike. Pansy seemed unimpressed with the scolding, and just flopped down in an immediate coma.

Relieved, Ginger headed back upstairs. She dried her hair, yanked on a silky green nightgown, dabbed on some moisturizer, brushed her teeth…and hit the sack.

She fell asleep before her head hit the pillow.

That restful sleep lasted maybe two minutes. The instant lightning streaked the sky and rain started seriously drumming on the windows, she felt something warm and wet and smelly touch her bare shoulder.

"No," she said firmly.

But then the damned dog started howling.

Ike stood in the pouring rain, hands on hips, staring up at the light in the far bedroom on the second floor. He suspected he'd scare the wits out of her—and Cashner—if they found a soaking-wet man in their house in the middle of the night.

But the problem was his dog.

Pansy had chowed down heavily in the morning, so he wasn't afraid she was hungry.

She also was happy anywhere, primarily because she spent so much time sleeping and she liked people in general. There were just a couple teensy problems with her temperament.

The main one, the worst one, was that she was terrified of storms. At the first shot of lightning, she'd been known to break through screen doors, let out immortal howls, try to fit herself under a bed. And she shook. Nonstop.

Bottom line… Well, he didn't know what the bottom line was, but he figured he'd start by seeing if the front door was locked. If the house was left open, it was a fair guess Ginger expected him to retrieve his dog.

He mounted the steps, taking off his wet windbreaker and hat on the porch…then did a rethink and took off his shoes, as well. No sense tracking in half a lake.

The door gave a slight creak when he turned the knob, but the sound didn't seem to arouse anyone. The only sound he heard was the tick of a pendulum wall clock, somewhere in that formal parlor. Silver rain streamed down windows, not letting in much light, but once his eyes adjusted, he could make out the tinkle-light of the hall chandelier, and the glow of a night-light at the top of the stairs.

He whispered, "Pansy!" which accomplished nothing. The dog had a great nose, but lousy ears. Like Ginger's grandfather, the dog could have benefited from a hearing aid.

He scratched his nape. Ike never liked making mistakes. He was ninety-nine-point-nine percent sure that going upstairs—even for the serious reason of reclaiming his dog—was a bad, bad, bad mistake. The only reason it crossed his mind was because the dog hadn't shown up so far. Which meant she wasn't downstairs. Which pretty much meant she was upstairs. Which for damn sure meant Ginger had been stuck with her since the start of the storm.

Amazing, how a man could justify making a mistake.

Still. There was a tiny chance he could retrieve the dog and hightail it out of there without waking her.

At the top of the stairs, he hesitated. Cashner had slept upstairs until a few months ago, when he and Cornelius had badgered him into making a move. The old house had plenty of spare space on the first floor. The room off the kitchen had once been a "sun room," with no particular purpose that Ike could see. A twin bed fit in there fine. A full downstairs bathroom was next door, so the location was ideal for a man getting older and less steady.

But the point was that the light on the second floor could only be coming from Ginger's bedroom. And she was alone upstairs. Which made it even more ticklish for him to go up there.

Out of nowhere, he heard a voice. "*Ike*. For Pete's sake, would you quit dithering out there and just come in and get your dog!"

The voice was very cross and very impatient. Definitely Ginger. And Ginger was definitely wide-awake, which made his conscience stop feeling so frayed. He quit dithering and hiked as far as the bedroom doorway. He took one look. His response was immediate and instinctual. "Uh-oh."

"Ike. Your dog is a complete and total coward."

"Hey, you didn't have to let her up on the bed."

"Right. I'm lucky she isn't under the covers. She tried." She was scowling at him—a pretty familiar expression, actually.

But he had to hold back laughter. Pansy was stretched to her full length, which meant she was about as tall as Ginger. The hound's face framed by the frothy-looking canopy over the bed was downright hysterical. Further, she was sleeping, eyes closed, snoring…except that her tail was wagging hard enough to shake the house.

She knew he was there.

She just wasn't inclined to move.

Ike could relate. Spooning next to Ginger in a storm on a chilly night… Oh, yeah, that sounded like a good idea to him, too.

He leaned against the doorjamb. "I would have called, but—"

"You left your cell phone in the kitchen."

"No. I mean, yes, I realized that. But I could have used someone else's."

"I figured that, Ike. I was thinking a lot of bad names about you this afternoon. Some of them were even eloquent curse words. But the bottom line is that I knew you wouldn't ditch your dog any longer than you had to. So you must have run into some trouble."

"I did. Tildey had two easy deliveries before, was so sure she didn't need more than a midwife. And I would have agreed with her, except that this midwife happened to be a twerp. Didn't know the umbilical cord was wrapped around the baby's neck. To top it all off, Tildey's two other kids, both under five, were crying and wailing and scared."

"So where was the dad?"

"Apparently he has a pattern of taking off to a bar when his wife goes into labor. Eventually he showed up…but right at the point when Tildey was a few huffs away from delivering. When she saw her husband, she tried to get out of bed, told him that she had a knife and if he ever touched her against she was going to use it."

"Oh, my."

"Then she actually produced the knife. It was in the drawer by her bed. A butcher knife. Belonged to her great-grandma. Made of straight steel."

"Oh, no." Her voice raised an octave. "*Pansy. Do not lick my face. Ever. Ever again.* Okay, Ike, then what happened?"

"The husband—Hamilton is his name—passed out. Crumpled right in the doorway. The midwife tried to step in, and Tildey almost turned the knife on her. She was just out of patience, out of strength, and she'd lost the rhythm of the contractions, just plain got screwed up. When she started crying, the kids started crying and carrying on, too. And that woke up her husband, who was as helpful as an elephant in a china cabinet."

She bunched the pillow under her head, turned

more on her side. The window lamp only provided a pale glow. He still couldn't see much of her face. Just talking to her, though, eased the long day's exhaustion.

"Are all your patients this exciting?"

"Actually…yeah. I don't see many gunshots or stab wounds or gang fight scars. Just straight life kind of problems. Anyway. Tildey had a son. Her two other kids are both girls. That's why they came easy as pie, she said. Men are always trouble. Even little men."

"Was the baby okay?"

"Absolutely. Bald as an eagle, a scream worthy of a rock band, a wriggling mass of furious baby boy." He eased into the room. Standing after all this time was exhausting. He just took a corner of the bed. The back corner.

"What color eyes?"

"Blue, silly. All babies are born with blue eyes."

"You think he's going to be cute?"

"Cute?" Ike had to think. "I'm not sure I ever notice whether a baby's cute or not. He looked healthy—and happy—once he'd been cleaned up and put in his mama's arms. Tildey settled down then, too. The kids saw the baby, but by the time the place was cleaned up, they'd cuddled on the couch with a blanket over them. I called the hospital—closest one is sixty-some miles—I didn't think Tildey has to get there until tomorrow, but the baby should be checked out."

"So she'll go?"

"She'll go. But I still couldn't quite leave that minute. She told me I looked like hell, to use the shower off the kitchen, which I did. I always keep clean clothes in the truck. Pretty rare they don't come in handy. I cleaned up as quickly as I could, but it was really late to call, and I was afraid of waking you both...."

"It's all right. I knew something had happened. However..."

"However?"

"Your dog, Ike, has no sense of boundaries. From the minute you left, she leaned on me as if I were a fence post. She moaned if I tried to go into the bathroom alone. Watched me while I brushed my teeth. And when she heard the first thunder—"

Ike winced. "I know."

"It was one thing for her to want to sleep near a human. I get that. I had nightmares as a kid. But she still wasn't happy until I turned the light on. And then she had to get in bed with me. I had to give her her own pillow, or else she was determined to share mine. If you don't do what she wants, she looks at you with that...face. Those eyes. That expression. As if you'd broken up with her. This is not a *dog,* Ike. She's a full-scale monster."

"I know, Ginger, I know. I didn't want her. When I moved here, she just showed up at the back door. I couldn't get rid of her. Tried to give her to a family down the road that had a bunch of kids. They loved her. But she came back. Tried to give her to the sheriff, thinking she could help, she's got a serious nose and all. He liked her right off…but she still beat me back home, and I swear, she takes all day to walk a mile. So I gave up. Anyway, I'm sorry she was such a nuisance."

"Ike. She thinks we're praising her. She's wagging her tail faster than a metronome."

Ike thought maybe they'd had enough of this chitchat. "I think she's got the best world she can imagine. Her and me on the same bed. With you. At night. Hell, it's almost foreplay, don't you think?"

The storm stopped. Just like that. No more thunder, no lightning, no silver rain tapping on the windows. The room went still as a stone. Maybe she hadn't noticed before that he'd slowly, carelessly sunk down on the bed. Just at her feet, not next to her. There wasn't room next to her, because of Pansy.

He'd leaned back on an elbow, at some point, because hell, it'd been a long day and it was late. And maybe he'd put a hand on her foot—which was covered up with sheets, of course. And maybe the embroidered sheet up near her neck had slipped a few inches—but only enough to reveal that she was wearing some kind of pale green nightgown.

The lamp by the window, he finally realized, wasn't an ordinary lamp. It looked like an antique, with an old brass base and a mother-of-pearl shade. Ike wouldn't normally notice details like that, except that the lamp wasn't…well… normal.

It had been the beacon that drew him upstairs, into her room, but that wasn't the issue. The lamp had magic. It had to have magic, because that soft glow made Ginger look irresistible in every way. Her skin, impossibly luminous. Her eyes, incomparably deep. Her hair, like copper on fire. And her expression…

"No, Ike," she murmured, but her expression wasn't saying no.

"No, you don't think this little meeting is like foreplay?"

"No. To what you were thinking."

"Ginger. There's a dog on the bed. I couldn't possibly be thinking anything that you'd object to."

"Yes, you could. Apparently no matter how bad I look or what the circumstances are."

"Now, Ginger. You're giving yourself an awful lot of credit for being irresistible."

"I am. Just that. But I learned the hard way that I only seem to be irresistible to the wrong men. Go home, Ike."

"Man. You can be really harsh."

There, that serious expression disappeared. She had to bite her lip not to laugh. "You're sitting on my bed, with this crazy hound, in the middle of the night! I'm not remotely harsh!"

"But it's just *me*," he said plaintively. "And

Pansy, of course. It seems really cruel for you to reject a helpless dog."

Rather abruptly, she threw a pillow at his head. That seemed to wake Pansy out of a dead snore. He made a tongue-click sound. The hound's eyes immediately opened, and graceful as a pregnant ox, she leaped down from the bed.

"I'm leaving," he told Ginger, still using his most plaintive voice. "But first, I'll turn the light off for you."

"Thank you. Good night. Goodbye."

He threw her another wounded look—as if she'd hurt his feelings yet again.

He crossed the room, switched off the light, took a second to let his eyes adjust to the sudden darkness. He knew where Pansy was. She never moved if she didn't have to, so she was exactly where she'd jumped down and waited for him.

Easy enough, then, to edge toward the bed.

Ginger sensed it, too. Said, "I mean it, Ike. No."

"Hey. I was just tucking you in." Which he did,

shaking off the sand Pansy had brought with her, easing the soft percale sheet under Ginger's chin, the light blanket beneath. Not touching her. Just tucking. And looking at her.

Swiftly—faster than a breath of wind—he bent over and kissed her. Just a light kiss. A texture to texture, taste to taste connection. At least he tasted it. The flavor of all that could be.

Just as swiftly, he lifted his head. "That was just a good-night-sweet-dreams kiss. So don't argue."

Ginger didn't fuss, but she woke up the next morning with a good fume on. By the time she changed the sheets—which happened to have a fair amount of dog hair and sand—she'd added to the day's fume. A shower, hair brush and fresh clothes later, the fume had become one of her best.

Ike was playing with her. Flirting, for lack of

a better word—and in the South, there probably was no better word, because the term had always been cherished below the Mason-Dixon Line.

She headed downstairs, reminding herself that she had a grandfather losing his mind, a pregnancy she hadn't even started to deal with, no job or means of supporting herself. So. There was nothing for Ike to be attracted to—which was why she was so certain he was playing. And the truth was, because she was stuck in a quicksand well of troubles, it felt good to do a little playing.

But that was no excuse to be so damned charmed by the man. He was a devil.

A rascal.

She found Gramps in the kitchen, wearing the same clothes he'd had on the night before, holding—for no known reason—a clock.

"Well, aren't you looking pretty this morning, Loretta," he said immediately.

She was in no mood to be patient. Not this

morning. "Gramps, this is me. Ginger. Not Loretta. I don't have a clue who Loretta is."

"You don't know where she is?"

She sighed. Made him scrambled eggs and toast, picked up the morning paper from the porch and sat across from him. "Gramps. Try to concentrate. What happened to Amos Hawthorne?"

"That old son of a sea dog? I fired him."

"Why did you fire him? Do you remember what happened? Do you know where he lives?"

Well, hell. That was clearly too many questions. He lifted his head and blessed her with a beatific smile. "These are probably the best eggs I've ever tasted in my whole life. You're spoiling me, honey, and I like it."

Okay, okay. She started answering to Loretta, got the kitchen cleaned up and tracked down her grandmother's old address book. Naturally, she should have thought of it first—but she quickly located the number and address for Amos Hawthorne. She put on shoes, grabbed a purse and was almost out the door when the landline rang.

Her grandfather picked it up, called out, "Ginger, it's the doctor. Ike. For you!"

She answered back, "Tell him I'm late for a meeting. Can't talk now."

"What meeting?"

"Just tell him, Gramps."

"But where are you going?"

"I told you. I won't be gone more than a couple hours—max. I promise. And you have my cell phone number."

She'd been through this with him several times. Gramps wasn't into technology like cell phones, and he didn't want to learn. Would probably forget it if he did grasp it. But she'd put her number on paper in several rooms so he could reach her whenever she was gone.

She tried calling Amos Hawthorne's phone, but no one answered, so when she climbed in her Civic, she plugged the address into her aging GPS and took off.

Amos only lived about ten minutes away, farther into the country, the sign for his road barely visible for all the scrappy brush. Once she located the house number on his mailbox, though, the landscape changed abruptly. Amos lived in a tiny white-frame house, but the lawn was manicure-perfect, the windows gleamed and even the driveway looked clean enough to eat off of.

She didn't try knocking at the house, because she could smell the burning brush the minute she climbed from the car. His property was long and narrow, and he'd set up a brush pile at the far back end. It struck her as amazing that he had any brush to burn, when every tree and bush and plant had been pruned to perfection. She'd known Amos from years ago—but he was distant from her life, never at the house, only someone who'd passed in and out of the tea store sometimes.

He was younger than Gramps by a heap, had taken the job when he was fresh out of school, but that was about all Ginger remembered about him. She thought he was tall—likely because she'd most often seen him atop a tractor—but he wasn't at all.

He was raking brush into his fire, and he half turned to fork up another small heap of twigs when he spotted her.

She was probably a couple inches taller than Amos. They probably weighed about the same. He was all wire and bone, with straw-colored hair, and skin prematurely wrinkled from endless sun exposure. He squinted at her.

"I'm Ginger Gautier, Amos. You probably don't remember me—"

"Shore I remember you." His voice wasn't unkind, but it wasn't welcoming, either. He poked the rake in the ground, leaned on it. Then just waited.

"I need help. My grandfather needs help."

"Cashner fired me. Told me I was the son of Satan. That I'd been messing with his wife." A scowl showed up, hard to discern from the rest of his wrinkles. "Your grandmother's been gone a while now. As if I'd ever have touched a hair on her pretty head. He couldn't have said anything to insult me worse."

"That's terrible, Amos. But my grandfather isn't in his right mind. I'm sure you must have seen changes in him. He really doesn't always know what he's saying."

"That's what you know. But I'll tell you what I know." He stopped the leaning on the rake posture, stabbed the rake into another short pile of brush. When he tossed it on, the flames shot up, and the smoke swirled in restless circles. "I knew he had trouble. And I got into it with him a while back, talked to him with all the tact I had. We needed to shut down the store. No one could handle it. The store was just a fun project for your grandmother anyhow. We could sell on the internet if he wanted to keep up that nature of the tea business. We could hire a kid to set that up. Even the dumbest kids seem to know everything about computers these days."

"That sounds like a wonderful idea."

"You think? Just suggesting that was when Cashner started cussing me out. That was the fight that led him to firing me."

"Would you consider coming back?"

"Why, shore…on the day it rains purple."

Ginger gulped. "What if I raised the salary you had before? And if you weren't working for my gramps, but me. And I'd be happy to accept your judgment on whatever you felt needed doing."

More stabbing brush. More sparks of hot fire. More simmering smoke.

"I don't like to turn down a lady, especially one asking for help. Lots of people with a farming background around the country here. But not many who know tea. But your grandfather treated me wrong. I understand. He's ill, so to speak. But I don't see being ill is an excuse for treating someone bad."

"I don't, either. But he's been calling me all kinds of names—like he thinks I'm Grandma. And some other names, I don't even know who they are. Amos, he's not in his right mind. I don't believe he'd ever have insulted you if he'd been himself."

"I don't know that. And I'm finding plenty to do. Everybody knows I did a good job at your place. That I work hard. Know my way around a wrench and a tractor. So I don't need that job anymore."

"Please?"

"I'm sorry. No."

"Even for a short period? Amos, I can't possibly replace you and really, really don't want to. But right now, I don't know a plant from a weed. Could you work with me for a while, just to educate me on things I should do, get some kind of idea what the place needs? I'd pay you anything you asked."

Ginger rarely met anyone as bullheaded as she was, but Amos wouldn't give in by even the slightest millimeter. She tried every guile and wile and coaxing that she knew. She even tried being flat-out honest. Nothing worked. After he'd given her his final "no" several times, she walked away…but she wasn't about to give up.

Amos had left her no choice but to try going behind his back. She walked the long yard back to the driveway—thankfully her eyes were stinging from the smoke, so her eyes were tearing. She had to look as if she'd been crying. She didn't try knocking on the back door, where Amos could see her, but approached the front door to ring the bell.

Amos's wife showed up, wringing her hands dry on a dish towel. She peered through the screen and immediately opened the door. "Why, honey, what's wrong?" she said. "You're Ginger Gautier, aren't you? I've thought a lot about you since your grandma passed. Did you have an accident? Are you hurt? Never mind, come on in, I'll get us some tea, and you can tell me whatever it is."

Guilt pinged at her conscience. Her grandparents had certainly never taught her to lie…but it wasn't her fault she had to resort to a little shady behavior. A girl couldn't sew on a button if she didn't have needle and thread.

She needed *some* way to coax Amos into working for her.

Chapter Six

Ike regarded one of his favorite—and most difficult—patients. "You know, Amos, it might help if you gave me a call before you were in a world of hurt."

Amos stuck out his chin. "I'm not one to complain to doctors."

"And I respect that. But gout is a mighty painful condition, and we want to address that uric acid before the numbers get so high. There's medicine that helps."

"Well, I know that. But I don't want any dang fool pills."

"Afraid you're going to have to bite the bullet, because I'm writing you a script for some of those dang fool pills. But I'm also going to recommend that we work on your stress level."

"I don't do stress and never will. I'm sick of everyone talking about stress as if anyone had a choice about it. Life's stress. It's just the way it is. And I need to work."

"But you don't need to work seven days a week. I want you to just try it. Relaxing. Take a long weekend with your wife, go up to Whisper Mountain, maybe camp out there or stay in one of the retreats or resorts around there. Sleep in. Take a couple fishing poles. Practice just sitting around and enjoying the view."

His patient looked at him. "Are you plumb crazy?"

Ike nodded. "What can I tell you? That's what they teach us in medical school."

"If I was to go up to Whisper Mountain, it wouldn't be to pay for any dang fool *resort*. There are stills in the hollows of that mountain. Moonshine. Good moonshine. Now *that* might help the pain."

"My family came from Whisper Mountain. My brother, Tucker, still lives up there. I've heard about the stills, but I figured that was just country legend."

"Nope. It's truth. When I was a kid…well, no, never mind. No reason you should hear about the wild things I did as a boy." Amos buttoned his shirt. "You know, this flare-up of gout happened because of the Gautier girl."

"Ginger? What did she do?"

"She went to my wife, that's what she did. Went around my back. I *told* her I wasn't working for the Gautiers ever again and that was that. And like I'd never spoke to her, she went to my wife, started crying, and the next thing I know, my wife is tearing a strip off my hide, yelling and not making dinner and making me sleep on the couch."

"No!" Ike tried to make his tone sound incredulous.

"You don't know my wife. She's kind to everybody in the whole county but me. She says I was being ungentlemanly for not helping that girl. That I was raised better. That her grandmother's passed and her grandfather left his mind somewhere months ago, and when that poor child asked for a little help, what did I do? Turn her down. My Lord. She went on and on. My back almost went out from sleeping on that old couch. There was no living with her until I agreed to help the Gautier girl, and I'm not just telling tales."

"Oh, I believe you. I've heard Ginger can be a little on the strong-willed side."

"She's pretty enough. But bless her heart, she's ornery clear through."

That was his Ginger, all right.

He hadn't seen her in four days, and that was about as long as he could take.

He was overdue a visit with Cashner, anyway.

Three patients later, he grabbed a bite for lunch and then he was free for the day.

Pansy howled when he gave her a fresh rawhide bone—she knew that meant he was leaving her—but a frisky wind was bringing in a fresh batch of clouds. The area needed more rain like fish needed feet, but Pansy'd do better at home in a storm than tearing around the country with him.

He turned onto Gautier property before two. One glance and he could see the place was starting to look better. The long, rolling lawn was freshly mowed, a lot of the tangled brush near the fence cleared out, and a dead tree had been cut down. He was still glancing at all the improvements as he knocked on the door—and then let himself in.

When he didn't immediately see or hear anyone, he ambled inside, aiming for the kitchen. He found a pot of Creole gumbo soup simmering on the stove, and more great smells emanating from a slow cooker. A stew, maybe? The air was rich with the scents of fresh basil and tarragon and pepper. A lot of great food—but still no bodies in sight.

Eventually he located Cashner, taking an afternoon snooze in front of the television. He did his usual prowl-around, checking the tray in Cashner's bedroom, making sure the medication was there and that Cashner was taking his pills. Normally Ike would have taken his blood pressure and pulse, but there was no sense waking him as long as his color was good.

Ginger's old Civic was parked in the drive, so she couldn't be too far. He checked the backyard, glanced around the garages—nothing. For lack of a better choice, he ambled across the road to the farm. A sharp wind bit at his sweatshirt, nipped at his neck. If it did rain, it was likely to be a mighty cold soak…which was probably why he noticed the wide-open door to the tea shop.

He'd never been in the retail shop before, had no reason to, but he knew that the tidy white building housed both the retail tea products and the farm office. Ginger's grandmother had done the landscaping herself, made the place pretty and welcoming from the outside.

When he stepped through the open door, though, he wanted to shake his head.

The inside wasn't just neglected; it was a disaster area. Dust and dirt carpeted every surface. The windows hadn't been washed in years. The stock on shelves was either in disarray or just suffered from an abandoned look. The old-fashioned cash register was gaping wide open. A mouse or some varmint had taken off with string and ribbon. Papers cuddled in corners and odd heaps.

But he'd finally found her.

Ginger.

On the floor, lying on her back with a bunched-up jacket behind her head.

He closed the door—since she hadn't had the sense to—and then hunkered down beside her.

She wasn't asleep. Her eyes were wide open and narrowed on him, her voice as cross as always. "How is it that you manage to always—*always*—show up when I'm at my absolute worst?"

Ike knew better than to answer an estrogen-loaded question like that. Besides, his first priority was to make sure she was okay. It didn't look as if she'd fainted or fallen, more as if she'd taken an impromptu rest.

Her appearance revealed that she'd been up to no good. She was wearing old jeans, dirty at the knees and seat. The white sweatshirt—well, there was a single spot, near her right shoulder, that was still white. The spot was no bigger than a quarter. The rest of the sweatshirt and everything else looked like something his mother would have thrown in the rag bag.

Her chin had some more dirt. Her hair had streaks of white, not from sudden age but dust. At some point she'd wiped her face and eyes with a clean rag—apparently—because there was an almost-clean swatch of face around the eyes.

But the familiar belligerence in her expression was enough for him to conclude she was fine. Frustrated and tired, but pink-cheeked healthy.

"So, is this really your worst?" he asked with pretend curiosity. "Do you promise?"

"Don't make me laugh, Ike, or you're likely to see violence." She closed her eyes tight. "Right now, Ike...I just plain can't see any possible way I could raise a baby."

So they were in the middle of that conversation, were they? "I don't suppose that maybe you're feeling overwhelmed because you *are* overwhelmed?"

Nah. She didn't like that answer. Didn't even try opening her eyes. "I don't have a job. I don't see any chances of a job here, at least in anything I studied for, and there's no way I could move away from here to find a job. I can't leave my grandfather for a completely unknown period of time. This is a royal, royal mess. And I just can't fix it. Or affect it. Not in a week. Maybe not in months."

He wished he could soften the edges for her, but there was no way. "Okay. What else?"

"Money. I don't exactly need a lot of money here. Gramps has enough coming in from Social Security and his retirement funds to keep him going. I'm not worried about him having enough to eat. It's just…"

"You don't have any spending money."

"Actually, I don't care about spending money. I had savings before I quit my Chicago job, and I have a few investments besides. My grandparents weren't about to raise any dumb granddaughters. But…" She sighed, still not opening her eyes. "But I still see huge debts possibly everywhere. I don't think Gramps filed taxes last spring. Amos says the fields are almost too far gone to bring back, and for sure there was no income last year. The farm could go under. And I don't know what the house needs to bring it back into good shape."

Now she opened her eyes, swung to a sitting position and sat cross-legged—which enabled her to hold a chin in one palm. "Ike, I need the legal right to pay his bills. To see what kind of financial trouble he's in. That's why I tried to talk to his attorney—crabby old witch that she is."

"She was just as complimentary about you."

"I kind of liked her."

"I do, too."

"But here's the thing. Even if I saw a heap of his records, I'm not sure I'd know what they meant. I've been all through the office in the house. Then I came out here. I was trying to go through everything—the inventory records and the tax records and the sales information and all that—but the place was so dirty, I couldn't even think. When my grandmother was alive, this place was spotless. And I found a bunch of records, but the numbers all started to blur in my head. And between trying to clean and trying to wade through gross and net numbers, I just got completely lost."

He got it. Why she'd been lying on the floor like she was in a coma. Or a wished-for coma. He'd likely have caved on line two of her list.

"Ginger…tell me about tea. This whole place."

"That's just the point. I don't know anything about the business! I keep telling you!"

She crashed back on the floor and closed her eyes again. He clearly needed a new tack. "I don't mean the big picture numbers. I meant… what are all these products on the shelves? White tea and green tea and black tea and all. What makes them all different?"

"They're not different. They all come from the same plant. *Camellia sinensis*."

"Huh?"

She opened one eye. "You're just humoring me, Ike. Trying to get me in a better mood. Trust me, I'm entitled to a terrible mood. I'd have to be certifiable to be in a good mood. There are no silver linings in any of these clouds."

"Okay. I promise you can go back to your terrible mood—I certainly would, in your shoes. But just tell me a little more. I don't get it. How you'd get all those different kinds of teas from the same plant."

She shot him a suspicious look. But she answered, "You always have to start with *camellia sinensis.* Then the next trick is to have the right climate, and to give the plants the right food and the right handling—to get the best quality tea. No shortcuts. No lazy stuff. No skimping on what the plants need."

"Got it. But you're saying that green teas come from the same plant that black teas come from?"

"Yes. Exactly. One tea plant could be bred a

little differently than another. But that isn't what distinguishes the type and taste of the tea. That's about how the leaves are handled. It's about fermenting."

"Fermenting? Are we talking about moonshine and stills here?"

"No, you goof. Tea's never alcoholic. But you get different flavors based on how you handle the leaves. You get white tea from picking the leaves before they're fully open, when the buds are still tiny and young. That makes white tea more rare. It's the most expensive."

"So…white tea is the best?"

"That's just a matter of taste. Green tea has a really light flavor. It takes a whole lot less fermenting—or oxidation—than the dark teas."

"So it's better?"

"Better is just a matter of taste. Green tea, for instance, has a really light flavor. The leaves for green tea aren't fermented—or oxidized—

at all. So those people who love green tea think the taste is more fresh, more herbal."

"How about you?"

"Ike. If you're raised a Gautier, all teas are holy. The worst sacrilege would be to not love tea. The second would be to believe one was better than another."

"Okay."

"So now we're up to oolong. You know what that is. Even if you're not a regular tea drinker, you've undoubtedly had oolong tea at Chinese restaurants. Oolong is between a black and a green tea. It's partly fermented—but not for a long period of time. Black teas are the richest, hardiest teas because they're fully fermented and oxidized."

"But then how do they get the other names? Like mint and jasmine and all that stuff—"

"You can add all kinds of ingredients to the leaves. Like you could add jasmine to oolong to make jasmine oolong. Or you could add mint, if you liked that spice. But if you preferred Darjeeling, for another example…Ike! What are you *doing?*"

Ginger knew perfectly well what he was doing.

The man was loco. Witless. In a complete meltdown. Marbles all lost. IQ dipping into the negative numbers. A major drafty hole between his ears.

He kissed her again, this time his lips just skimming hers before sinking in for a long, slow kiss.

Daft. The man was daft. She was filthy. Buried in dust and paper and discouragement. Hadn't brushed her hair in hours. The tea store was a romantic setting on a par with…

On a par with…

On a par with…

She couldn't think. He suddenly twisted around, shifted them both so that he was flat on the floor now and she was propped over him.

It should have been awkward, the sudden tangle of arms and legs, both of them off balance. But his mouth never severed from hers. It was a whole swoosh of sensation, her breasts against his chest, the heat and pressure and throbbing of his erection against the soft cradle of her pelvis.

That gasp of awareness…she wasn't expecting it, had had no idea the fierceness of longing and need were so close to the surface. Longing for him. Need for *him.* How could she have known?

Possibly the real problem was that she was kissing him back.

Possibly he wasn't the only daft one—but she had excuses. She was exhausted. Worried. Anxious. She'd been trying so hard to do the right things, to make something of her life, to stand up for doing what needed doing…and every time she turned around, even more insurmountable problems seemed to show up.

Besides which, Ike was a wicked-good kisser.

Crazy. But lunacy didn't affect the parts of him that worked really, really well. He had certain beguiling habits. He surprised, but he didn't pounce. He took, but she just couldn't see it coming. He was a lazy man who brought every ounce of laziness to his kisses, as if every taste, every scent, every sensation needed to be examined and savored. He touched. Her upper arms, her back, into her hair, down her spine, around. Every stroke, every caress, conveyed the tenderness of a man who could soothe a lioness, disarm a wild animal.

She was going to slap him any second.

Pretty soon.

Any second now.

That lazy trick shouldn't have worked. She'd never liked lazy or slow. She always galloped, never walked. Her temper was a brush fire, quick and hot, then over. It was who she was, how she was.

Except with him.

He pushed up her sweatshirt. Slid his hands into her jeans, pressed on her fanny, so she was glued even tighter against him. Still, he pulled kisses from her.

Still, he made her close her eyes, because she felt so shivery and weak. Still, he made sounds, volatile sounds, groans, murmurs that sounded a whole lot like a love song.

"Ginger."

"Hmm?" She lifted her head, but not willingly. She opened her eyes, but only reluctantly.

And there was reality, in the form of his rugged face and unshaved chin and devil-blue eyes. He sucked in some oxygen. Smiled at her.

"I'm all about this," he assured her, and then said it a second time, because his voice didn't seem to carry any volume on the first try. "I'm more about this than you can imagine. But at least the first time…I think we can do better than a dirty floor. A place where anyone could come in. Where there isn't a pillow or a candle in sight."

She pushed up. Scowled at him. "We were never going that far."

"No?"

She sort of straddled his thigh, trying to get off him. Everything that had been so impossibly right…now seemed so impossibly wrong.

Ike told himself he couldn't be falling for her. He just couldn't. She almost kneed him in his privates in an effort to scramble off him.

But damned if she didn't look adorable. Still dirt-smudged. Still rattled. But there was still passion in her eyes, an earthy pink in her cheeks. Women liked him. Women had always liked him. But she sparked something different for him, something dangerous, something compelling. Maybe because she responded to him as if he were the only man in the universe—at least her universe.

"You're not looking happy," he murmured.

She was still straightening, tugging, smoothing. Sunlight streaming from the windows glowed on her face, put fire in her hair. "I'm definitely not," she agreed.

"You mad at me?"

"No. I'm mad at me."

Her voice was still cross, but he relaxed. "I like that answer. I was hoping I wouldn't have to apologize or grovel."

She stood up, pushing a hand through her hair as her gaze swept the tea shop. As awful as it was, Ike could see there were patterns to her messes. One mountain was trash. Paper piles were separated into taxes and receipts and similar records. A trash barrel held broken pottery. Unbroken tins and tea containers were temporarily shelved together.

"I don't suppose you know how to fix a broken antique cash register?" she asked, as if they were in the middle of a completely different conversation.

"If it's old, then it's not electronic. If it's just a mechanical problem, there's a slim chance I can." He uncoiled, stood up. He'd seen the cash register gaping open, just hadn't bothered to wonder why. But now he tested the drawer, and shortly discovered the obvious. Something was caught behind it. He leaned over, tried to reach in. "We're going to need a tool. Knife. Screwdriver. Fork. Something long and thin."

She went on a search, came through with a long-handled spoon.

He took it and she said, "Just be a little careful with it, okay? It's sterling silver."

He rolled his eyes, gave her back the spoon.

"It was all I could find!"

"Think ruler. Tape measure. Fly swatter..."

She found a ruler. He swore. She played cheerleader. He considered asking if she wanted to talk about it... It seemed fairly monumental to him, nearly making love in the least romantic place on the planet, no foreplay, no warnings, just a kiss leading to Armageddon. But then he figured she'd bring it up if she wanted to, needed to.

Eventually—by half killing himself—he managed to figure out the problem. Two acorns. Some shredded paper. Some unmentionables. "You had a mouse make a nest back there."

"Ew."

"That's an elegant way to put it." He tested the drawer two more times, making sure it closed and reopened cleanly again.

"Ike...it's not easy for me to ask a favor from anyone." She'd thrown out the debris he'd unearthed in the register, pulled hand sanitizer from her pocket and liberally used it on her hands—then offered it to him.

"Well, I like the idea of your asking favors from me. Then you're in my debt. That's always good."

She chuckled, but there was a carefulness in her tone. "I need...well, I need someone with

me next Thursday. I have to talk to Amos Hawthorne, on the tea farm, about the tea farm. We
set up a time. But since I'm not his favorite person…"

"How could that possibly be? When you're so
cute and smart and so easy to get along with?"

A ball of wadded-up paper hit his forehead.
"All right, all right, so it might be my fault that
Amos isn't too fond of me."

"Because you went behind his back and sicced
his wife on him?"

She glared at him. "That could be part of it. But
the point is that he's coming to talk on Thursday
afternoon. Three o'clock. And you may have patients, I realize. But if you're free, I'd appreciate
your being here."

"You feel you need protection? That he might
strangle you?"

"Well, I'm hoping it won't come to that. I'm
going to practice being meek and agreeable. But
just in case I can't pull it off…"

"You'd like backup."

"Yes. If you can. And if you wouldn't mind."

"Well, this is an easy yes. No sweat. I'll be here a few minutes early." He was amazed at the workings of the female mind. At least her female mind. He'd probably have paid gold for the chance to be there for her. And extra platinum for her asking him, specifically him, to play a hero role for her. Casually he mentioned, "You're using me."

"I know. I know. It's not nice."

"That's okay. Feel free to use me whenever you want."

She looked as if she was about to reply when his pager went off. He was tempted to throw the damn thing in the river. Every time they got into an interesting conversation, he was interrupted.

"I have to go," he said. En route to the door, he managed to swoop an arm around her waist and peck a fast, soft kiss on her forehead. "Be good. But only when I'm not there, okay?"

She bristled up, but he just laughed. And dug in his pocket for his truck keys.

Chapter Seven

Ginger paced in front of the farm office at the speed of a Derby contender. Ike was late. He said he'd be here by three on Thursday, and it was three minutes after three.

She'd been ready for Amos Hawthorne's arrival since before lunch. Not that she was nervous, but she couldn't eat anything but a few soda crackers with weak tea. She'd pitched and tossed clothes because she couldn't find a pair of pants that buttoned. She'd still had a waist until that morning! Suddenly the pooch had appeared.

The pregnancy had been on her mind every other second for weeks now—she wanted to make decisions, forge plans, positively hated procrastinating about anything so serious. It was just that Gramps's issues were more immediately overwhelming. He was the crisis. She couldn't be the crisis until she had time to be the crisis.

A truck turned in the drive. An old pickup, which made shards of anxiety twist in her stomach—it wasn't Ike, but Amos, and she'd so counted on Ike being here first. Clouds clenched and darkened in the west. Since it typically rained a ton in the fall, another shower wouldn't be unusual, but she needed at least an hour with no rain. She needed to win over Amos. She needed the darned farm taken care of so she could go back to the rest of the crises in her life.

She needed an awful lot to go right over the next hour.

Amos pulled into the drive, stepped out. She

had the old golf cart with the canopy top all charged up and ready to boogie—which he'd asked for. It was the easiest transportation around the acreage. "Thanks so much for coming," she started to say.

Amos greeted her with a scowl darker than the sky. "My wife sent you a pecan pie, seeing as she thinks the sun rises and sets with you. Just so you know it's from her and not from me. I don't appreciate your going round my back to my wife, missy."

"Please thank her so much for the pie. And I'm seriously sorry, Amos. I know what I did was wrong." Her voice was sincere. She was willing to eat as much crow as Amos wanted. If he'd just help her.

"Yeah, well, when I say no to something, I mean no. The only reason I came is because I thought about it, and realized it was your grand-father that fired me, not you. So I'll fill you in on how things are. Explain some things I know you don't know. Then you can do whatever you want with the information. I'm out of it."

"I'd appreciate any help you could give me." She'd practiced that contrite voice, hoped she sounded subservient and meek.

"Well, let's go." He motioned to the golf cart, took the driver's side, took off the minute she was seated. His first stop—his priority stop— was in front of the major field of tea plants. "All right. What do you see out there?"

She looked. She'd seen the view a million times. Green as far as the eye could see, that unique rich green of tea plants. Nothing looked dead. The field exuded an exuberantly fresh and unique smell.

"It looks healthy to me," she said carefully.

"Then you never looked real close, did you." Amos didn't phrase it like a question.

"I wasn't ever looking from your eyes, Amos. But it's true. I have no memory of what the fields looked like in October."

"Well, I'll tell you how it looked when I was managing the place. The top of that field should look absolutely even. Floor-even. Table-even. There shouldn't be a branch or a leaf of a limb sticking out anywhere. This is a mess."

She gulped. "I guess my first impression was that the plants looked healthy."

"They are healthy. Those plants will live another few hundred years. Never had trouble with them," he said fondly. "One of the nice things about tea is that you never have to use chemicals like insecticides. No insects anywhere around here. Nobody knows why. Some say that the insects don't like the natural caffeine in tea. But whatever. If you're good to a tea plant, it'll last centuries and more."

"You love them, don't you, Amos?" He was starting to calm down, at least a little.

"You think I worked all those years just for a paycheck? Of course I love it." He started driving again, but slowly, pointing out this and that.

"You see a bald eagle over head, you know it's one of the farm's. Bald eagles like it here. There's always at least a pair nesting by the irrigation ponds. When the young are born, they bring them to the tea plants. The plants are so close, the trunks so gnarly, that no predator can get in there. The mama can go out hunting, knowing her babies are safe."

"Gramps showed me a nest one time," Ginger murmured. "I thought those babies were about the ugliest, scrawniest hairless critters I'd ever seen." She hoped to coax a smile, but Amos took off again, his posture stiff as steel.

"You know how many tea plantations there are in the United States?" he demanded.

She shook her head.

"Three. There's one way bigger than ours, right in the Carolinas, a lot bigger name than we have. They make great tea, sell it all over the world—but that's all right. What we had here was our own little taste of paradise. We never wanted to be big, just wanted the best tea in the universe. The best tea is all in the plants. Nurturing them as if they were babies, giving them the perfect food, just the right amount. You have to know every plant as if it was a kid of yours. See any bad behavior, you have to stop it in its tracks. But you have to love it, too."

She looked at him, suddenly realizing that she'd misunderstood the situation completely. She never had to win Amos over. It wasn't about her. It was about the land. And her grandfather should have given Amos a serious piece of the land a long time ago.

"Amos," she started to say seriously, but then stopped. From the corner of her eye, she saw a pickup—a white charger of a pickup—turning from the far, long side of the field. Her heart thumped even before she could identify him. So he was a little late. He'd said he'd come and he had.

He was the lover she couldn't have—which

she'd known from the get-go. But tarnation, he did stir her blood like a burst of light after a long dark storm.

Ike, being Ike, took his time getting out of the truck and ambling toward them. He shot her a look—but to Amos, he extended a hand. "How's the gout doing, Amos?"

"Could be better. Could be worse. I'm not complaining."

"Good to hear. And the wife?"

"I thought that cough was going to never stop. The medicine you gave her helped a smidgeon, I have to say."

Faint praise, Ginger mused. Still, it was obvious that Amos trusted Ike. She could see it in the way he shook Ike's welcoming hand, how he stood taller, how a hint of a smile showed up.

Before they'd stood there two minutes, though, Amos drew a line in the sand. "So, Doc, I assume you showed up because you're riding shotgun for Miss Ginger here?"

"Well, I'd have to admit to that…except the truth is, I don't know anything about your business, the tea, the land, any of it. So I'm likely to keep my mouth shut."

Amos turned back to her. "Well, I'm not through telling you things you need to know."

"I'm listening," she said, and added "sir" with all the Southern feminine syrup that she'd grown up with. The sky started spitting rain. It wasn't a lot, wasn't even a drizzle, more like a slow drool with a plop landing here and there. Just enough to make her hair frizz and her neck feel sticky.

Amos abandoned the golf cart and led a walk around the acres that would have exhausted a marine. The greenhouse. The pump. The supply barn. The irrigation setup. The warehouse where the harvest was brought in, first to the withering bed, then to the rotovane, then to the oxidation bed.

"What's wrong in here?" he asked her, the same as he had, at every stop.

The answer was always the same. Her. She was the one who was wrong. Her lack of knowledge was adding up to a college degree in ignorance.

"What's wrong," Amos prodded her, when she failed to express the correct answer, "is that the machinery's just sitting here. Not turned on. This place should be busy and noisy, the last harvest of the season. The greenhouses should be filled with cuttings started during the growing season. There's nothing right happening anywhere on the premises."

She felt a hand at the small of her back. Ike. Who hadn't said a word or offered a question or anything else. He was just...there.

"Amos," she said carefully, "are you trying to tell me the only solution is to sell the property? Is it all so far gone that it can't be brought back?"

"That's your business and your grandfather's. Not mine."

"I would still value your opinion."

"Well, you could sell the place. But not for tea.

Not going to find anybody who knows about tea. And as far as selling her for general real estate…she's a pretty piece of ground, so I guess some developer might look at it. In this market, though, I'd doubt you'd get value for your money."

She gulped. So far she hadn't heard any good news. "All right. So the next question. Is it possible to make it viable again? To bring it back."

"Well, sure. But it'd take a trunk full of money."

"How much money?"

"Honey, I don't know."

"But I'll bet you have a general idea. I suspect you'd know more than the bank would about a problem like that," she added.

"Well, that's another for-sure. People wearing suits don't understand land. About no one understands tea." He pulled a bag from his pocket, looked at her as if silently asking her permission.

She had to shake her head. The bag held chewing tobacco. She was about positive if he started chewing, she'd hurl…and then this whole afternoon would be for nothing. "Please just throw out a general figure. What you think it'd take to bring it back."

"Well, it's gonna take a year of no profit to bring it where it should be again."

"I understand."

"You'll have to pay for the work. And a lot of the work has to be done by hand when it's been let go to this point."

"I understand."

"She could make a good profit. She always has. When you make the best of something, there's always a market for it. But your grandmother had the gift, and she's gone. Your grandfather did his time, but you know he hasn't got the judgment of a rock any more. And then there's you." Amos shook his head. "You couldn't do this, missy. You're too soft. Too much to learn. You're too much a city girl."

She almost bit his head off. She wanted to. She could. She knew perfectly well when she was being insulted—and she knew exactly how to lose her temper because she did it so often.

But damned Amos. He was telling the truth. It wasn't a truth she wanted to hear, but of course, he was right. She couldn't possibly handle the farm herself. And there was no one else.

Ike spoke up for the first time in a blue moon, his voice casual and easy. "Amos, could you just throw out some kind of dollar figure to Ginger? Just ballpark. Just something that would give her an idea what kind of money it might take to turn this around."

Amos looked at Ike, not her. "I don't know, I'm telling you. I mean I've seen some figures. I know what some things cost. I know what I used to be paid. But I can't guarantee—"

"Aw, Amos. We're not asking for a guarantee. Just a ballpark number. If you were running the place, what would you think it'd take to put the land back on firm footing?"

Amos scratched his neck. "Well, I dunno. But I'm saying a hundred grand easy. That'd be the drop in the bucket. But I'm guessing it'd be more like two."

"Two hundred thousand?" Ginger echoed. All right. It wasn't as big as the national debt, but it might as well have been. For a second, only a second, her eyes squeezed closed. Who knew? Who could possibly have known that she could conceivably feel this sharp-sad sinking feeling of loss?

She'd never dreamed of being part of the working tea farm. Neither had her grandparents. Neither had anyone. She was just trying to find solutions for her grandfather's situation. That's all. But realizing her family could lose it all brought on a heartsick so sharp she could hardly swallow.

She heard a buzz, realized it was Ike's cell. She

felt his gaze on her face, hawk eyes, assessing…
but he turned around to answer the call.

He flipped the cell shut in less than a minute. "I'm sorry, Ginger. It's the one problem
with being the only doctor in town. It's sort of
a twenty-four-seven thing."

"You have to go," she said.

"Yeah. Seems a five-year-old had a fall from
a jungle gym. Sounds like the child's fine, but
the mother's a wreck and a half."

"Of course. You have to go," she said. And
meant it. But not really. She'd never wanted to
be the kind of woman who needed a man in that
capital-*N* way. But right then…well, she did. She
wanted to lean on him. On Ike. Not any man.
Just on him.

If a woman's world was falling apart, well,
then, it was. But she just wanted a little company.

She felt him squeeze the back of her neck, a
tender gesture, almost a whisper of a gesture—

but then he turned away and hiked toward his car. And she was left to turn around and face Amos alone.

"I want you to thank your wife for the pie, Amos," she said sincerely. "I'll write her a note myself, but please let her know how much I appreciate it."

"I will," Amos agreed, and propped on his straw hat again. Apparently he thought their meeting was over.

So did she. But somehow, words came out of her mouth that she'd never planned on. "Amos, if I could get that money…and add to the salary you once had. Would you be able to bring the farm back?"

"Someone could. If they stepped up now, and no later."

"But you could do it. If we had the money… you could do it."

Amos narrowed his eyes at her. "Don't you go talking to my wife again, missy. You went behind my back once. I won't forgive it a second time. You can bat those pretty eyes at the doctor, but not at me."

"Yes, sir."

"The answer is no. And I won't say it again."

"Yes, sir."

By the time Amos left, Ginger wandered back home in a funk…and the rest of the day deteriorated from there. Sarah-Just-Sarah had left chicken and dumplings, homemade, absolutely delicious—but somehow her stomach couldn't tolerate it. She lost that, snacked on soda crackers, which stayed down but were hardly comparable to a great cook's recipe for anything.

And then there was Gramps. He'd had a good morning, she knew he had. But when she sat down with him at dinner, tried to talk to him about the land, the tea, what Cashner believed was happening with the property…her gramps just kept smiling at her, saying that she looked prettier every day, that she shouldn't be worrying about things like the farm, she should be thinking about going out dancing with some nice young man…although he'd beat her at gin rummy if she had nothing better to do.

By eight-thirty, Gramps had retired to his room. Ginger prowled through the empty house for a while, eventually poured herself a Darjeeling, and headed outside to the porch swing.

The drizzling rain had long stopped, but the dark clouds refused to move along. The evening was unrelentingly dreary—a perfect atmosphere, Ginger figured—to indulge in a good long wallow in self-pity.

It wasn't as if she didn't have plenty to feel sorry for herself about. She considered crying—nothing she normally indulged in—but hey, when a girl was miserable, she might as well go for it whole-hog. As she explored how awful things were—how awful her life was, how impossible her entire future was, how she was failing right and left to achieve any of the dreams she'd had as a young girl—she almost worked up to some serious crying.

But then she heard the sound of an engine coming in the drive. She didn't look up. It couldn't be Ike driving in, because fate couldn't be that unkind. Practically every single time he'd seen her, she'd been at her physical, mental and emotional worst. And part of the reason she was considering a long, noisy, blubbering crying jag was specifically him.

She'd wanted him to stay during the confrontation thing with Amos. She'd wanted him to save her. She was sick of being a mature, capable woman. She wanted the prince to charge up on his white horse and make all the awful stuff go away. She didn't care if there was a happily ever after.

She was pretty sure there were no happily ever afters. But she still wanted the stupid prince and the white horse.

While her eyes were still closed, she was

forced to realize that an animal had shown up on the porch. Not a white horse. But the bloodhound, who leaped toward her and immediately tried to clean her face with her long, fat tongue.

She reared up, and instead of yelling at the dog, she put her arms around the damned hound and hugged her. Pansy sat down and accepted the affection as her due.

Eventually she had to look up. Or look at. Ike hadn't sat down, more hunkered down to be on eye level with her. Behind the clouds, the sun was dropping, adding more gloom and gray to a night that was already fuzzy and dim. He looked at her as if she was under bright lights, though. As if the only thing in his universe was her.

Because she was a damn fool—hopefully not forever, but for now—all she wanted in that single zinging moment was to make love with him. As if that would solve anything. As if that could mean anything.

"How was your patient?" she asked.

"The kid—Jacob—was fine. The dad almost required a tranquilizer. The mom was visiting family out east. She's pregnant again, and he thought she needed a break, so he offered to take care of Jacob. He's a good dad. He just keels over at the sight of blood."

"Uh-oh."

"After Jacob, I had a snakebite to treat. An old granny who should have known better. Found a copperhead on her front porch and decided she'd just get a rake and move him off."

"Not?"

"Not. Copperheads aren't the most poisonous of the snakes around here, but they're not a dip of ice cream, either. Her blood pressure shot to the moon."

"She's okay now?"

"Yeah. It just took some time. How'd the rest of the meeting with Amos go?"

"Oh, it was even more fun after you left. Amos said it'd take somewhere between one and two hundred grand to put the place in shape. But he wouldn't do it. And no one else probably on this continent really knows much about tea. And he was still mad at me for talking to his wife."

"Wow. I missed all that?"

"What can I tell you? You missed all the best parts."

"Two hundred thousand, huh?"

"Yup. I was thinking of driving into town, picking up a lottery ticket."

"I don't know. Afraid then you'd need two hundred thousand and one."

"Plus gas."

"Yeah, forgot the cost of gas. So. That meeting with Amos make a few things easier for you?"

"Easier?" She kept petting the dog, kept trying not to look at Ike. She'd afraid he'd see the yearning.

"Yes. You never wanted part of the tea plantation yourself, right? So now you know. Selling it's your best option. You don't have to sweat feeling like you lost something that mattered to you. You never wanted to be in the tea business."

She sucked in a breath. Who knew that hearing the words in Ike's gentle, easygoing voice would make her feel slapped? Which wasn't Ike's fault. It was true...she'd never wanted anything to do with the tea farm. Ever. Until Gramps had said someone was trying to take it from the family. And then she'd come here and realized that her whole family history was about to disappear, all the love and family lore and memories of the house and land and people...unless someone else could take it on.

"I'd have to be downright stupid to try to keep it," she said hollowly. "I have a degree in business. Not farming or agriculture. I started out wanting to be in medicine, veered off into business and hospital administration. Might be hard for you to see it, but I was darned good at my job. And loved it besides."

"Hey. I suspect you'd be darned good. You're

smart. And you're more than fearless when you take something on."

"Some things, maybe. But not agriculture."

"That issue's moot, isn't it? Since you don't want anything to do with the tea farm."

"I *know* it's moot. I'm just saying…you probably don't think I could handle something like the farm. Because I'm so unqualified and all that."

"Hey. That's like worrying whether you can shoot an Uzi. It doesn't matter since you'd never volunteer to try it."

She had no idea why she suddenly felt it rising. Temper. She'd been depressed and anxious and wallowing in self-pity—but not mad. Not remotely mad. Yet she knew all the symptoms. Bristling energy. Itchiness. Couldn't sit still. And the smell…trouble always had a tantalizing smell.

She pushed off the porch swing, lifted a hand to Ike as if she wanted to say something or make some gesture…and then just didn't. Instead, she stalked off the porch. Pansy, with an extremely reluctant groan, forced herself to her feet and tore after her. For the hound, a walk was a walk. Even if it was an inexplicable hike around the house at seventy, seventy-five miles an hour.

She didn't see Ike get to his feet. Didn't hear his footfalls in the grass. But suddenly she heard his voice just behind her, lazy as the night breeze.

"Did I miss something in the conversation?"

"No, of course you didn't."

"You took off like a bat out of hell. What's wrong?"

"Nothing." She stopped, swatted a bug nipping at her ankles. Took off again.

The backyard glistened with rainy leaves and smelled like a rain forest and was just as dark as her fitful mood.

"Okay. I must have said something to upset you."

"No. Of course you didn't. What could you possibly have said to upset me?"

"I have no idea. That's why I asked." He added kindly, "You seem to be letting out steam from both ears. I'm pretty sure you're ticked about something."

"Well, I'm not. Pansy just needed a little walk." But Pansy, the lazy turncoat, apparently decided that two times around the house was more than enough exercise. She heaved herself back on the front porch and threw herself on the welcome mat.

"That's okay," Ike said in the same annoyingly kind tone. "You don't need the Pansy excuse. I'm up for as many laps around the house as you need."

She stopped dead, parked her hands on her hips. "Would you stop being nice to me?"

"Okay. Just say it, then. What the problem is."

"Which one? I seem to have about five million right now."

"The one about the land, Ginger."

She was tempted to sock him. Even though

she'd never hit anybody and was a firm believer in taking out her temper only on inanimate objects. Still, she put some serious fury in her voice. "I can't save the darn land. There's no possibility. I'm too ignorant. The learning curve's too steep. And the day I could convince a bank to loan me two hundred grand will be the same day pigs fly."

"But that's not the point," Ike persisted calmly. "That'll be the point tomorrow. Tonight the only point is for you is to say out loud what you really want to do."

"Good grief, you're exasperating. You want me to say it, I'll say it. I hate to give up the land, the tea. It's my whole heritage. I didn't think it remotely mattered to me…but it does. My grandma loved it. My mom loved it. It's part of who I am. The part I always knew I could come home to. It's home, in a way no other place could be. Now. Are you happy?"

"Oh, yeah," he murmured. "You did good."

And as if the man hadn't behaved like a lunatic since he got there, he suddenly grabbed her. She was half in shadow, half in the porch light. She saw something in his eyes that made her suddenly want to shiver.

And then of all the fool things to do, he kissed her.

Chapter Eight

Ike almost hadn't stopped by. He knew Ginger'd had a challenging day, and he'd been going nonstop since daybreak. But once he turned in the yard...well.

Maybe he'd wanted to be sure she was okay. Maybe in some place in his heart he'd known this was going to happen. A kiss, just like this one.

She fired up faster than a rocket. And he kept telling himself he felt resentful for the way she so easily rocked his world. Everything had been fine until he met her. Now nothing was.

Yet he felt the energy of a superman when his lips touched hers, claimed hers. The kick was fast and potent. It didn't matter that they were standing in the middle of a rain-soaked yard. It didn't matter that Pansy was up on the porch snoring. It wouldn't matter if the sky cracked open and rained daisies.

Nothing mattered when he kissed her. And that was the whole thing.

He felt rich with her. Rich on her. Her lips were expensive, sheer-soft, yielding.

She sank into him when he kissed her, at least when he kissed her until they were both breathless, and that's the only way he seemed to know how. Her body bowed into his, obviously made for him, because all the right parts touched. Breast. Pelvis. Heart.

She gave out a swish of a groan, a woman sound, angry—darn it, the woman was always angry—but it was still another yielding. She liked to be kissed. At least she liked to be kissed by him. That shot up his testosterone level another notch, and desire had already put his hormones in the stratosphere.

"Hey," he murmured, hoping she'd think he still had some sanity left and would listen if she objected.

But she didn't object. And she ignored his token *hey*. She suddenly lost all patience with his shirt, pulling and tugging and wrestling with it. Once her bare palms found the bare skin of his back, though, she slowed down. Just...stroked. Rubbed. Made catlike sounds of pleasure. She snuggled her lips against his neck, nestled in against his bared chest, rocked.

"Ike," she murmured.

"Hmm?"

"I wish you wouldn't do this."

His eyebrows arched. She had a habit of making comments that left him speechless. Maybe he'd initiated the kiss, but she'd responded whole hog, rocket speed, shooting past all the stop signs. He hadn't made her do that. He hadn't made her do anything.

He eased up, not too far. Her hands were still on his back, his hands looped around her neck. Foreheads touched instead of lips. Both practiced breathing.

"There's this really nice lady," he said.

"Oh?"

"Her name is Sandy Joe. She makes me cakes all the time. And cookies. And brownies. She's two years younger than me. Divorced about four years. As comfortable to be with as an old pair of gloves."

"I'll bet there's a reason you're telling me about this woman."

"There is, there is. I like her. She's a good person. Kind. Sweet. She's been waiting for me to ask her out for months now."

"Um, are you hoping I'll give you advice about that? Like 'Dear Abby' or something?"

"No. I'm just saying. I've wanted to ask her

out. She couldn't be nicer. And I couldn't figure out why I didn't just do it."

"I'll bet you want me to ask why."

"You don't have to ask. I want to tell you. It's because of you. I didn't realize there wasn't a pinch of chemistry when she comes around. But any time I'm near you, I'm ready to go off like a firecracker. In principle, it doesn't make sense. You've got a mean streak. You're difficult. Contrary."

"Yeah, but you're forgetting the obvious factor, Doc. You know I'm not on the market. It's a whole lot easier to let the sparks bubble to the surface when you know there's no...repercussions. No risk."

"You think there's no risk? Of my falling for you?"

For an instant, he saw the glow of something perilously vulnerable and soft in her eyes. "You didn't say falling. You were talking about chemistry. Sex. Sparks."

"The hell I was," he murmured. He almost turned to walk away. Almost. But it was that vulnerability in her eyes, the disbelief that he could actually care, that sent him in another direction entirely.

He pulled her close, tilted his head, kissed her hard this time. He wanted to give her sugar, not hot pepper. Care, not roughness. She had so much on her plate, so much she was trying to cope with. He wanted to give her tenderness, empathy. He felt those things.

But somehow it all came out with heat and flame. He kissed her bruising hard—she moaned and twisted tighter in his arms, met fire with fire. Everything that was impossible between them came out in an explosion. Her fingers clutched his shirt, then yanked at it, a button popping, her meeting every wild kiss with another, until he couldn't breathe and she couldn't breathe and neither cared.

Soft shadows danced into darker shadows.

She pulled him off balance, not intentionally, but he had to twist swiftly in front of her so she wouldn't fall under him. The crash was awkward…silly. But she wasn't hurt. He was the one flattened onto the wet, cool grass, with Ginger scrabbling on top of him. He almost laughed, even regained a pinch of sense, said, "I'm pretty sure that was a sign we should both signal a no…"

But she whispered right back, "I'll let you know when I'm saying no, Doc, and it sure isn't now."

This couldn't happen. He knew it. There wasn't a prayer of their making love, not here, not now, not on wet grass with the night whisking up a chill breeze. It was out of the question.

But when she tumbled on top of him, he assumed she was scrambling to climb off. Instead, she turned the awkward position into temptation, straddling him—straddling him tight. For that first millisecond, her eyes were above his, a silky hint of moonlight illuminating soft, wet lips and the sharp flare of emotion in her gaze. He'd seen the vulnerability before…but not this kind. This was the naked kind. She was upset and mad—nothing new about that with Ginger—but she didn't seem mad at him.

She seemed to want to lose herself in him. Forget everything else. Ignore everything else. Make the whole darned impossible world disappear. She dipped her head, closed her eyes, took a kiss—and that was a capital-K, estrogen-fueled, woman-wicked of a kiss. Her tongue found his, and her body started rocking against him, inviting, coaxing. He was already steel-hard and hot, and her soft, warm flesh against his was not helping.

Her hands found their way past his shirt, rubbed against skin, ribs, chest. Her mouth took another soul-stealing kiss while those busy fingers of hers sneaked down, lower, below his navel.

There was a line Ike figured every woman ever born knew better than to cross.

She'd crossed it.

He might be on the bottom, but he couldn't wait another second before getting his hands on her. Her top pushed up. Her pants pushed down. She was a long, slow stroke, from her midback to the valley at the base of her spine, to her delectably small little butt. She groaned, softened a kiss against his neck.

"I don't want to hurt you," he said.

"You couldn't."

"Ginger. You're sure this is what you want?"

"I'm sure that I'm sick of trying to do right things. Sick of decisions. Sick of worrying and all that other nonsense. I just want to *live* for a moment, Ike. With you. Feel. Experience. Lose myself. With you. Is that okay?"

For bare seconds, she lifted her head, sought his expression in the shadows. He didn't answer. Couldn't. She did look lost. Crushable.

A woman who'd had all she could take, at least for a while. And if she wanted him to be the answer, hell…

He'd have climbed mountains for her. Given her probably anything he had and then some.

Making love was an easy yes. In spite of the night's damp chill, her skin was fever-warm… more so when he scooched off his jeans, pushed her pants down to thigh level. A rock dug into his back. His whole backside was soaked through. Smells permeated the night—the verdant earth, bark, grass, sweet leaves. Her.

He arranged all he could arrange, held her hips in his palms…whether he slid into her, or she climbed on, he wasn't sure. Didn't care. Seduction was never all that fun unless it was an even-steven sport. Her smile was sudden and glorious, a little shocked—he loved that, that the feel of him inside her, owning her, claiming her was rich enough to shock her. She went weak all of a sudden…but that was more than okay. He felt richer than Croesus, watched her face, felt her whole body build up tension and need…and too soon, way, way too soon, watched her peak with a sharp, sweet cry.

He seemed to be breathing louder than a freight train. She sank on top of him with all the strength of a limp noodle, nuzzling her face into his neck. That moment, that exact moment, was so good. Beyond any good he could recall. She was his, the way it never mattered before. He wanted her, no one else. Loved her, like no one else.

Eventually, she rubbed her cheek against his shoulder and then eased up on an elbow. She touched his lip with the tip of a finger. Looked about to say something when they both startled at a sudden voice.

"Annabelle!"

They were deep in shadows, but even so, Ginger peeled off him faster than a gunshot. He jolted aware and awake as fast as she did. Both of them buttoning, zipping, straightening—and sharing a look of laughter.

They were both standing up and reasonably respectable by the time they spotted Cashner, the kitchen light behind him, standing on the back porch in his undershorts and a saggy tee. "Annabelle Marie, you come in the house! You get away from that boy this minute!"

"Gramps, it's me. Ginger."

"And I'm the one out here with her, Cashner. Ike."

"I don't care who either of you say you are. There's a dog howling on the porch. A lovesick hound. Woke me out of a sound sleep. You're grounded forever, Annabelle."

"Who on earth is Annabelle?" Ike whispered.

"I haven't a clue. I think he's adding girlfriends to his imagination. He's not forgetting. He's just inventing people now and then. Most of them seem to be women."

And to her grandfather, she called out, "I'm

coming, Gramps. And Ike'll take Pansy with him. Everything's fine. We're all going to sleep now."

Maybe they were, but Ike wasn't.

She thought she was no risk. That he had nothing but sexual feelings for her.

Ginger's father had taken off, or so the town always said. And the doctor she'd fallen for sounded like another take-off-for-where-the-grass-was-greener kind of guy. Somehow she'd started seeing that as a man's default position. When a guy had to show up for more than fun, he took off.

Ike wasn't that way.

He'd never been that way.

But that didn't mean he had any answers for a woman with serious trust issues.

He drove home with Pansy leaning her extremely heavy head on his shoulder, which meant drool slobbered down his shirt—which meant he'd need to shower before climbing in bed. He could have stopped the dog from leaning, of course. But it was Pansy's thing—sticking close when her human was upset.

Ike wasn't necessarily admitting he was upset. He didn't get upset. He'd never had a nervous bone in his body. A guy who had two high-powered surgeons for parents learned the hard way, mighty young, that panic in a tough situation accomplished nothing. But he hadn't liked leaving Ginger after making love. Hadn't wanted to leave her at all that night…much less after a crazy melding in that rain-soaked yard. He wasn't sure what she felt…about making love. About him.

But for darn sure, their whole relationship had abruptly become more complicated and precarious than before.

Minutes later, he pulled in his driveway—and let out a deep, tired sigh. A battered, mud-painted Jeep was already parked in the drive ahead of him. There were times he valued company. This wasn't one of them—even if he happened to love this particular visitor. Pansy lifted her head, but didn't waste the effort of barking.

She knew Rosemary.

Every light in the upstairs was on, the front door unlocked. He could hear his washing machine running, and at the top of the stairs— blocking the way—was a duffel bag stuffed with dirty clothes. It was easy enough to track down his sister. He found her—as always—crouched in front of the refrigerator, taking out covered dish after covered dish.

"About time you got home," she told him. "And man, I should have stopped by a lot more often than this. You must have every single woman in the county cooking for you! Good grief!"

"It's not my fault. I don't know how to stop it. They never ask. They just show up. Or I get home to find a covered casserole on the porch." He claimed his hug, then zipped out of sight as fast as he could. It didn't take him long to shed the wet clothes and pull on old sweats. Rosemary readily picked up the topic of conversation.

"It's just because you're cute. And you're a doctor. Every Southern mama's version of a catch. Except for the hound."

"Hey, Pansy's the best chaperone there is. She starts drooling and the women backtrack toward the door."

"Not me," announced his sister, who not only greeted Pansy with a kiss on the brow, but offered the dog chicken divan. From a fork. She did stuff like that to get his goat, because—she claimed—that's what sisters did. Worked hard to drive their brothers crazy.

Judging from the heap of dishes on the counter, she'd already had sugar pie and a piece of Coca-Cola cake—before heating the chicken divan. She did the same thing to Tucker—the oldest of the clan—showed up when she wanted feeding. But Ike's fridge always had the best goods.

She looked okay, Ike assessed. Her blonde hair was still shorter than grass, her face tanned and freckled, and she hadn't gained an ounce. Late last spring, just days before a big-to-do wedding, she'd called it off and taken off. No one knew what she'd told George, her ex-fiancé, and the parents were still fit to be tied. Just after that, Rosemary had disappeared up on Whisper Mountain. Well, maybe not exactly disappeared, considering she was a botanist and had a two-year grant to study wild orchids in the region.

But she was living like a hermit, out in the wild. There was a mountain-top cabin, adequate shelter but not a place meant to live in. It was rustic, no amenities. She showed up—either to his place or Tucker's—when she needed clothes washed or some serious food. Or, being Rosemary, to reassure her brothers that she was okay.

"You were the one who got the brunt of our absentee parents, weren't you?" he asked.

"Sheesh. Talk about diving into deep waters before we've even done the dishes."

"I'm just saying. Tucker and I are guys. Most of the time we didn't mind fending for ourselves. But you were the girl. Whenever you needed a dress for a prom or the right shoes before school or a permission slip to go somewhere… you needed Mom. Not two brothers who didn't know a curling iron from a lipstick."

"Did you ever hear me complain?"

"No. But you also never told anyone why you really called off the wedding."

"Listen, you." Rosemary had experience pointing a fork at brothers. "I didn't come here to be badgered. I came here to do the badgering. I heard from Tucker a couple nights ago."

"Any news?"

"No. He's still sounding like a lovesick goon. I can hardly talk to him. He's happy about this, happy about that. He started singing on the phone."

"Oh, no. Not that."

"Yeah. Like that. I usually check in with him once a week when I'm on the mountain, but I can't stand listening to all that sweet stuff. And then I checked in with the parents."

That made him pause, study her face. Their parents had been gung-ho on her marrying George and had given Rosemary a major hard time ever since. "So…what'd they have to say?"

"Pretty much the same message I get every time. They're certain I could still make it up with George, still get a wedding going again. If I just called and talked with him."

"And you probably said, *oh, wow, thanks so much for that advice?*"

By then she'd finished gorging herself, spun a kitchen towel into a weapon and smacked him. "So," she said firmly, "what's the deal with you?"

"No deals. Just the usual. My life's good. Love being the town doctor, love that every day's different, that there's always something unexpected around the corner. It's a good place, good people."

"Uh-huh. So who's the woman in this picture?"

"I'll be darned. Did I mention a woman?"

"I'm your sister. I can read between your lines any day." Rosemary cocked her head—her hair looked like a sun-streaked mop, her eyes too-searing blue. "It's not someone from town. I knew you'd never get the itch for a small-town girl. You do the laid-back thing really well, but underneath, we're all stuck with the parents' overachiever genes." Abruptly she jogged over from the sink and checked out his face close up. "I'll be damned. You're actually seeing someone."

"I never said that."

"You didn't have to. I'm looking at your face. Good grief, you've got the same goon expression that Tucker has half the time. You've got that secret smile. You're distracted. You just put a dirty dish away in the cupboard."

"I probably do that now and then."

"No. You don't. Ever. Wow. Wait until I tell Tucker."

"When you were a kid," he said heavily, "I beat you up now and then. I still could, you know."

"That went the way of urban legends. You never beat me up. You were an amazing brother."

He changed tactics. "I agree. I was beyond good to you. So why would you pick on me now?"

"Just tell me her name and I won't ask a single other question, I swear."

"Oh, yeah. I believe that like I believe there's a man in the moon."

"Aha. There *is* a woman in your life. Come on. Spill."

That'd probably happen in one or two zillion years. Ike didn't spill. Didn't talk personal stuff the way his sister loved to do.

But just for a second, he wanted to. All teasing aside, he trusted Rosemary the same way as he trusted Tucker. The MacKinnons had always stood up for each other. He wouldn't mind getting Rosemary's take on Ginger's situation… like whether it was fair for a guy to push—for a relationship, for risk—with a woman who was under so much stress. Whether he was nuts to think the two of them could make it. Whether Rosemary'd think he was even more crazy to have fallen for a lady who was carrying another man's baby.

But he didn't.

There was no point in telling Rosemary. He already knew those answers.

He needed to stay away from Ginger. To let her breathe. Let her figure out what she wanted and needed. Pushing her—the way he knew damn well he wanted to push her—was wrong any way he said it.

But that was going to be extra hard, if not impossible, after making love with her.

Ginger had barely buttoned her favorite pants—a light green that went with an equally favorite cotton sweater—when the button popped. Actually it popped like a bullet, soared to the far window, ricocheted and then rolled under the bed.

She turned sideways in the bedroom mirror, and there it was again. The new pooch. Not a watermelon or a basketball or anything that huge. But the stomach shape had changed from concave to convex. Just like that.

In case she wanted to postpone dealing with the pregnancy issues, her silhouette was a caterwauling wake-up call.

She retrieved the button, yanked her hair back in a low tail and aimed downstairs. Just like that, on the third stair, she remembered Ike. Ike in the moonlight, kissing her. Ike, like a flash of magic, suddenly spinning her troubled world into a soft, whimsical place, where the power of the right man and the right woman could handle anything, fix anything, conquer anything.

She'd believed that last night.

She could believe anything when she was with Ike…but more, so much more, after they'd made love.

Impatiently she put some steel in her spine. This was a real-life morning. It had to be. And all her life she'd fought allowing herself to believe in dreams and magic—for seriously good reasons.

Her dad had been a nonstop believer in magic, a dreamer who was always sure there could be a pot of gold at the road's end. When she was little, her dad could talk her out of nightmares with his whimsical stories. And her dad was the reason she should never have fallen for a smooth-talking doc. She knew about smooth-talking dreamers.

She just never wanted to be one.

Ike was nothing like her Chicago ex. She knew that. But her twisted, goofy, inexplicable feelings for Ike were darned scary. Steve had introduced her to some strong feelings. Ike—well, Ike was an earthquake, a tsunami, a cataclysmic explosion of emotion. There was no comparison.

Ike was far scarier.

She just needed some space away from him for a while. It wasn't as if she had to invent reasons to be unavailable. She had problems crashing down on her life in every direction.

She grabbed a mug of tea and an apple, then tracked down Gramps. He looked bright-eyed this morning, was standing in the library with binoculars. "C'mere, Ginger. I think I spotted a bald eagle."

"Really? Let's see." Gramps handed over the binocs. The creature was across the road, close to the irrigation ponds, perched on an overhanging limb. It was definitely an eagle. A young one. "She's adorable," Ginger murmured.

"I think it's a boy."

"As if either of us could tell from here." She grinned—Gramps grinned right back—and it was so good to share this kind of moment with him again. They'd always taken joy in the simple things in nature. "You busy?"

"At my age, I don't know what busy means any more."

"Then would you take a short ride with me?"

He had trouble getting into her old Civic, and then he grumbled about having to wear a seat belt, but it was obvious he liked it—going out with his best girl, as he put it.

"Do we have a destination?"

"Oh, yes," she said. The first stop was for an ice cream cone at Willie's—the best ice cream in the universe, even on a cold morning. And Gramps had always been a sucker for chocolate velvet—Willie's specialty. From there, she drove back home, but instead of turning in the house drive, she turned into the tea plantation.

She'd finished her single scooper, but Gramps was still lapping on his double cone when she put the car in park and turned the key.

"Pretty morning," he said.

He knew something was coming. Knew the minute she turned in the wrong drive. When Cashner was thinking clearly, he was undoubtedly smarter than she was ten times over. "We need a serious talk," she said. "Do you want to stay here?"

"Until I finish my cone."

"Gramps. Don't joke. Is this where you want to be, to live, for the rest of your life?"

"I won't live anywhere else. This is home. It's everything your grandmother and I worked for. Lived for. Every best memory I have is here. And those sure include you, honey."

She nodded. "Same here, Gramps. I love you to bits. But we have some financial issues. If you want to stay here, we have to find some way to make money off our tea again. I could learn all I can, but I don't believe that's even close to enough. If you want to stay here, we have to find a way to rehire Amos."

Cashner finished his cone, wiped his hands on the handful of napkins she'd brought him and shot her a shrewd look. "That'll happen when hell freezes over. He insulted me."

"And from what I hear…you insulted him."

"He tried to tell me what to do!"

She wasn't sure how long she could count on him to have a clear mind. "Here's the whole picture, Gramps. If we're going to live here, two things have to happen. We have to rehire Amos. And we have to find a way to coax the bank into loaning us a boatload of money. They're both long shots."

"Sweetheart—"

"No, please, Gramps. Just listen. If we can't make that happen…then there's still no worry for you. You'll be with me. Wherever I am, you can live with me, stay with me." Those were big promises she was making, Ginger knew well. She hadn't a clue how she was going to make a living, not right that minute. Much less did she have a plan for handling the pregnancy and earning a living at the same time.

On the other hand, first things came first. The most immediate thing that needed securing was Gramps.

He stared bleakly out the window, then turned back to her. "I couldn't leave here, Loretta."

She swallowed. Once "Loretta" or any other name came into play, she knew his mind was fading to a different place. "Every memory you love, Gramps, is in your heart. It doesn't matter where you are. You have all those memories. They're yours forever."

"You're talking foolishness, honey."

Foolishness, she thought, was for that afternoon. She couldn't imagine anyone at the bank responding to her loan request with anything but downright laughter.

By the time she took Gramps home, he was ready for a nap. She tried a light lunch, and then called the bank to set up a time when the bank manager might be free. The response was a sweet trill of laughter.

"Why, bless your heart, but you don't need an appointment around here, sugar. Just come on in. But before four-thirty, mind you."

That pretty much cut out any chance to pro-crastinate, so she headed upstairs and foraged for clothes. She had a work wardrobe from her Chicago job, but none of that was quite right. She needed lucky clothes. A feel-good blouse. A little jewelry, not pizzazz-y stuff, but maybe one of the gold pendants that had belonged to her mom. And makeup. Afternoon makeup, not going-to-a-party paint, but still. Serious lipstick. Tidy eyebrows. A wink of blue earrings, to go with the wrap-neck silk blouse, black slacks that were slimming and comfortable. She went so far as to force her feet into heels she hadn't worn since Chicago.

She'd barely walked through the front doors of the People's Bank of Sweet Valley before realizing she wasn't dressed fancily enough. The bank manager was a woman. Ginger could smell her perfume all the way from the manager's office, past the tellers, past the lobbies, to just about the front door.

It was a nice perfume. It was just sort of gob-smackingly strong. Lydia Trellace came out to greet her, wearing suede pumps and a two-tone suit. Her champagne coif had been shellacked so precisely that a tornado wouldn't likely bring it down. Diamonds winked from her ears, her watch was a whole circle of them and on a delicate chain at her throat she had another rock that likely made her neck ache by the end of the day.

Lydia's office had also been decorated within an inch of its life. No sterility here. Two massive vases of fresh flowers flanked the desk. On the walls hung a variety of oils, likely painted by locals—or flowers done by someone who had a heavy hand with pink. A pair of chairs was upholstered in a pastel tapestry print, and the carpet was a thick wedge of ivories and pinks.

"I knew when you said the name that you were Cashner's granddaughter, honey. Sit down and I'll pour you a little sweet tea. Tell me what I can do for you."

Ginger perched at the end of the chair. She'd rehearsed something to say at home. Obviously she couldn't come right out and beg for a couple hundred thousand dollars, with no collateral of her own, and her grandfather too not himself to provide any of the management or knowledge the tea plantation needed.

Still. Her stomach was steady. She'd been getting serious rest. She couldn't stop the stress cooker she'd been stirring around, but she hadn't had a dizzy spell since that first week in town.

She was ready, she told herself, but somehow she ended up blurting out, "Lydia, I need a bank loan for two hundred thousand dollars." The response from across the desk was a stunned silence.

Ginger didn't need a crystal ball to suspect the bank manager's response of speechlessness was not an auspicious sign. But once her request was out there, she had to follow through and fill it all in. "Lydia…it's not known in town or anywhere else, but I'm going to have a baby. I want to raise the child here, on the land that belonged to my mom, and her mom, and her mom. I wish I'd known my grandfather was having trouble coping, but I didn't, not until a few weeks ago." The room started spinning. She ignored it. "The farm needs work and money to make it viable, but there's every reason to believe that can happen. The tea plants are strong and sturdy. Until my grandmother passed away, the farm made a great living. It's a special place, not like anywhere else in the country. Once it's gone, all that heritage would be destroyed with it. It'll be at least a year before we can start talking any kind of return. But…"

"Honey, take a breath."

At some point in Ginger's long monologue, Lydia had reached for the desk phone. She called Ike. Who else? There was only one town doctor, and it wasn't as if Ginger could have cut her off at the pass. She wasn't finished talking. She just happened to finish her explanation from the carpet, which was plush enough to feel almost comfortable. The chair really had been spinning. The carpet was staying in place. As long as she didn't close her eyes for too long.

"Here's the thing. From your side of the fence… why would the bank want the farm? In today's economic times? What would you put there that could make you a solid investment? Houses? You know that's not a good idea right now. And the tea…the tea plants can grow for hundreds more years. It only takes a couple people—and of course, all the machinery, but we already have that—but overall, it's a low-cost setup. We can do this. It's a good investment. I know, I know, you're thinking I have no background in agriculture. That I've never spent time in the field at all. And you're probably wondering about Amos because none of this would work without a farm manager, but I think—I'm almost positive—I can get Amos to come around. The thing is, first I have to be able to tell him that we're a go. That the farm is a go. For that matter, I talked to Gramps's attorney. Obviously I can't do anything without having his power of attorney and all that—and I don't yet. But that will happen because it has to. Gramps really can't take care of himself right now or pay his own bills. Amos is the one who said a hundred thousand, max of two hundred thousand. That's only because it'll take hand labor at the start. I'm sure you'll need a bucketful of paper and past records to give me a positive answer. I understand that. But I still had to initially talk to you, to find out if there was even any possibility of—"

"Ginger," Ike said calmly. "Stop talking. Open your eyes for a minute."

She'd already opened her eyes, the instant she felt his warm hands on her wrist, felt…well, she'd felt his presence. She didn't know when that happened. When she started just *knowing* when he was around. It was a primal thing. A sixth sense. A warming in her bones. A zooming in her blood. Even before she actually laid eyes on him.

"I'm fine, Ike." Except for last night showing up front and center on the big screen in her mind. All it took was looking at him. His being this close.

"Believe me, I think you're way, way, way more than fine." His humor was as wicked as his smile…but the smile faded awfully quickly. "I do think you're okay, Ginger. But we're going to have to do something about the stress load you're hauling around."

"I sure agree. Do you have a magic wand you could wave around, or something like that?"

"Not on me. I'm going to cart you over to the office, though. Do some blood work."

"I'd rather do the wand thing."

He didn't even blink. "We'll get the blood work done, then see if I can cook up a wand from somewhere."

He was so damned adorable. All that gentleness in his eyes, all that easy-don't-worry smile in his voice, all that sex appeal. Even when she was on the carpet. In a bank. With nothing remotely sexual on her mind. "Ike, I need to finish talking to Mrs. Trellace."

Lydia abruptly showed up in her vision. Apparently she'd been standing by the door since Ike arrived. "Honey, you just go with the doctor now. You gave me enough information about the loan you want. I can put some questions and paperwork together."

"But—"

"There really wasn't going to be much more we could talk about today, sugar. I don't care how big or small the loan might be. I'd need time to work with a financial plan. You just go on with the doc now, honey."

Ginger started to sit up—or tried to.

It wasn't as if she had a choice—but that didn't mean she liked it.

Ginger liked being forced into anything like she liked Brussels sprouts.

Not.

Chapter Nine

When Ike walked in with Ginger under his arm, Ruby was sitting at the reception desk with a phone glued to her ear. She glanced up, took one look at him and then a fast, shrewd look at Ginger. That fast, she put a hand over the mouthpiece and started rattling off information. "I just put Mrs. Barker on hold. I can deal with her. Mr. Black went home, said he'd call you back in a day or so. Merline came up for her blood pressure check. One of those annoying drug people stopped by, wanting you to try their new antihistamine product, put those samples in lockup. George Moon's mother called, she's bringing him in, said he got into another fight and a kid hit him on the head with a rock, he's bleeding."

"Just another day in paradise," Ike said to Ginger.

"You don't have time for me. And I feel much stronger now," she told him.

Yeah. As if he was going to let her loose. He had her safely tucked against his shoulder, and that's where she was going to stay until he had her upstairs. "We already did the 'I'm okay' conversation, so don't start. Ruby, I'm taking Ginger upstairs, need to do the vampire thing, then put her in a recliner by a telephone. Tell me when George and his mother get here, okay?"

"Will do. Nice to see you, Ginger, honey."

"You, too, Ruby. Although I'd appreciate you telling your boss that he's behaving like a Neanderthal."

Ruby put on a smirk and kept it there. "I totally

agree with you, sugar. But you don't know doctors like I do—especially this one. There's no
point in arguing over the little things, because
your whole day'd turn into a quarrel. With all
men, you need to pick your fights, dear. Sitting
in a recliner for a few minutes doesn't seem all
that bad, does it?"

"Sitting in a recliner is one thing. But what on
earth difference does it make if I'm sitting by a
phone?" Ginger questioned.

Ike responded to Ruby. "Ginger was just at the
bank. In the course of a conversation with Lydia
Trellace, she let out that she was pregnant."

Ruby sucked in a breath. "Oh, my." She
glanced at the wall clock. "The whole town will
know before four-thirty."

"So Ginger's likely going to want to call her
grandfather pretty immediately. Get a correct
story out there."

"I don't have a story. For heaven's sake. This

isn't the Middle Ages. I'm not a scandal just because I'm pregnant."

Ruby looked at her fondly. "You must have forgotten that you're below the Mason-Dixon Line, honey. And Lydia, bless her heart, got an A-plus in plays well with gossips in the sandbox."

"But I don't care what Lydia tells anyone."

Ike slipped in a word. "But you do care what your grandfather thinks. And you don't want him hit with personal family news coming from outsiders."

That silenced her immediately.

Ruby stood up. "I'll bring up the blood tray. Anything else?"

"Nope. And I'll be back down as soon as George and his mom get here. That's all for the afternoon?"

"Martin said he'd stop by after work. No appointment. He wants another refill, thinks he can talk you into it." Ruby added something else, which Ike couldn't hear. Pansy must have suddenly realized he was home, because she let out a bloodcurdling howl of welcome and galloped in from the back porch to greet them, and then tried to trip them going upstairs.

He climbed behind Ginger, with his hands on her waist. He told himself he was worried about her losing her balance, but that was just a politician's truth. He was worried about her. That was more true. He'd already run tests, knew her numbers were terrific…but one way or another, she wasn't fainting again. Not on his watch.

And that was the real truth. Ginger was on his watch. He knew perfectly well that didn't mean as a doctor, but as a man.

He'd fallen for her. Every termagant ounce of stubbornness. Every leap-to-conclusions impulsiveness. Every born-to-argue gene. At the moment her face looked washed out, with none of her normal sassy color. Didn't matter. She was beautiful that way, too. That way. Any way.

"Park," he said, once he'd steered her into

the living room and his old leather recliner in the corner. It wasn't a big room, but it had a balcony and enough space for both his leather couch and chair. The flatscreen was on the north wall. Wood blinds closed out the heat or the light when he needed to.

"Well, aren't you the bossy one. Maybe I don't want to sit down right now."

"You need a bathroom?"

"Oh, for Pete's sake. If I did, I could find it on my own."

She was extra crabby when she felt vulnerable. He'd thought that the first day he met her, but he knew it to the bone by now. She sank into the leather chair with a don't-you-mess-with-me-buster expression…but she'd curled her legs under her and leaned her head back about a millisecond after she sat down.

"Blood work first," he said. "Then when Ruby's gone, we talk."

She looked as if she was about to give him another argument, but Ruby knocked and showed up in the doorway with a blood work tray. After that, he started talking about how beautiful, how exotically unique, how breathtakingly exciting her veins were. Ruby started laughing at him, and that provoked Ginger into laughing, too. The blood draw didn't take him more than a couple of minutes, including asking Ruby to send it off to Charleston with his lab order. He did general testing in his own lab downstairs—but not for the fancy stuff.

Not for Ginger.

Once Ruby left, she immediately started talking. "Ike, I want to know what you're testing me for. Do you seriously think there's something wrong with me?"

He answered the question about the tests from the kitchen, where he poured a long glass of sweet tea for her and foraged for some crackers. He juggled the snack on a plate and set it on the table by the landline phone. Then he hunkered on the ottoman in front of her. "And no, I don't think anything's wrong with you. I also don't like putting pregnant women through unnecessary tests, especially in the first few months. But we need to be sure you're not fainting for a health reason. I'm certain the reason is stress, because that's the obvious conclusion to come to. You're carrying the weight of several elephants on your shoulders. Ginger…"

She took a sip of tea, then snuggled deeper into the oversize chair. "I know. You think I should tell my grandfather about the pregnancy. But I don't agree with you. You know the shape he's in. The last thing I want to do is confuse him with any extra problems."

"I understand. And maybe you're right. But I think there is another way of looking at this. Cashner is increasingly lost in his own little world. You might actually help him by giving him something else to think about, to worry about. Something besides himself."

She fell silent with a frown, obviously considering that idea. He gave her a minute, then slowly pushed into the sticky area he doubted she wanted to talk about.

"Back to the stress subject. Sarah can help take cooking and kitchen chores off your hands. And we can get your outside work done, because Jed could make a jungle look like a manicured golf course. But I have the impression you're trying to save the world here. At least your grandfather's world."

She frowned again. "That's not true—or fair. Decisions have to be made. My grandfather isn't capable of coping. I have to make sure he's taken care of. And that includes what happens to the tea. I can't just leave Gramps with the mess he's in, and there's no one but me who can step in."

"I understand. But let's break this down into more manageable parts. Do you want this baby, sugar? Yes or no."

She sucked in a breath. "Yes."

He said, lazylike, "You're sure."

"I wasn't sure before. But I am now. Yes."

"So you're not trying to jeopardize the pregnancy by taking on all those elephants?"

Her jaw dropped. "No, Ike. *No.* I didn't ask for any of these elephants. I came here and found them all in the living room, so to speak. I don't know what the right thing is about anything. But I'm trying to face the situation head-on, make whatever decisions have to be made. So if you're criticizing me—"

"I wasn't criticizing you. I think you're a trouper, doing great at figuring it all out. It's just…a ton."

"I know."

Since they were already swimming in murky water, he figured he might as well push a little deeper. "So," he said, "have you told the baby's father?"

She squinted at him. He was coming to think of that expression as her ornery look. He was trespassing where she hadn't opened any gates. "No."

"Why not?"

"Because when I took the first pregnancy test, it seemed too soon to tell anyone. I needed time to think about what I needed and wanted to do before going public. Especially with him. Calling him was never going to be easy. So I wanted my ducks in a row."

"So…that was then. But this is now."

He got another of those looks, and figured he was risking being slapped upside the head. But then…she apparently decided to answer. "This is now," she agreed. "And the man I thought I was honestly, deeply in love with…is probably on his honeymoon with the upper-crust lady he married."

Ike knew the story had to be upsetting. But from his viewpoint, he was relieved to get the past guy finally out of the closet and in the open. How could he know if he had an enemy, a rival or a saint until Ginger was willing to share what happened? "Okay. So he's a royal jerk. But if he's the father, he's the father. You have every right to financial child support. And I would assume he has every legal right to see the child."

Her arms crossed. "Exactly who's asking these questions? Ike the man…or Ike the doctor?"

"Damned if I know. All I know is that we need more of those elephants out of your living room. And this is the biggest one. Our being able to talk about your pregnancy. About your situation. Figuring out what those issues mean for you. And for me. And for us."

"Oh."

"Oh what?"

"I had no idea there was an 'us,' Ike."

Wow. That stab in the gut felt as real as a knife blade. Which was stupid. She'd come here, fresh from a hurtful relationship, doing a complete start-over of her life. She'd never implied she was looking for a serious relationship in any way. He'd come along; they'd slept together. What was this, the nineteenth century? He had no reason to assume she took the two of them as an exclusive pair.

He'd have to be stupid to think that way. She wasn't his girl. His woman. His fiancée. His significant other.

But damn it. He wanted her to be. All those labels and a few more.

"Ike, I can see you don't know what to say. I'm not trying to—"

"Don't sweat it." He knew how that sentence of hers was likely to end. No, she didn't want to hurt him. Yes, she wanted to give him a kick in the teeth…but she wanted to do it nicely. So he'd say thank you.

Thankfully, Ruby paged him. "Get down here, Doc. George is here and he's bleeding all over my desk. And the mother brought the baby and a neighbor's baby, because there was no other babysitter. And they're crying all over the place, too."

"I have to go downstairs," he said to Ginger.

"Of course you do."

"Just keep your feet up for a few minutes. This shouldn't take forever."

He wasn't sure whether she looked more relieved—or he did. But for damn sure that conversation hadn't gone well, and dealing with screaming kids had to be easier.

Pansy usually raised a fit if kids were in the place and she wasn't included, but right then, the turncoat looked perfectly happy leaning her full weight against Ginger's easy chair.

Downstairs...well. George was six. An extraordinary hellion. The kid was scrawny, so the other kids made fun of him, and George had seemed to decide in preschool that he was resigned to regularly fight. Besides the ripped shirt, the kid had a face full of dirt, scuffed-up knees, a bruise on his cheek and a scrape cut on the back of his leg. Ike liked the kid from the get-go.

Virginia Moon, the mom, was one of those mothers who did the Rock. She couldn't stand still. She was too used to having a baby on the hip or the shoulder, so she automatically seemed to start that rocking motion. "The problem, Doctor, is that I can't even discipline him for fighting. Because he comes home hurt. And Tom, that's my husband, he says a boy has to stand up for himself, and that's just what George is doing, so I should just leave him alone."

Ike finished cleaning the scrape-gash on the back of George's leg, and then plucked out a tray of assorted Band-Aids. The adults got the boring stuff, but the kids could choose from an array of cartoon and hero character bandages. George knew the drill. He knew where the lemon drops were, too, for the kids who did their best to be brave and not cry. Or cry. Whatever. A kid got a lemon drop if he wanted one.

Then came the problem of addressing tag-along babies. They weren't just crying to drive George's mom crazy, in spite of what she said. The one baby—the one that Virginia was care-taking—had an ear infection, so that mom had to be phoned and a script called in to the drugstore. Once the noisy bunch left, Ruby started closing up and Ike took on the aftermath cleanup.

Ike made it upstairs before five—just before—but as soon as he turned the knob he realized there'd been no need to hurry. Ginger was still curled up in his recliner, with Pansy sleeping at her feet. One of them was snoring excessively. It wasn't the redhead.

He stood, just looking at her for a good long while. Late-afternoon light was a pale wash of yellow, making her hair look brushed with pastel fire. She'd dressed extra businesslike for the meeting with the banker, but curled up, her black slacks showed off the soft curve of her hip, and the blue silky blouse showed her throat and the satin swell of her breast. The tidy hair…well, Ginger's hair was never going to stay sculpted back and tamed for long. Strands and curls were scattered on her cheek, her throat, her forehead.

There was no sign of the ornery Ginger right now. The fighter. The obstinate, crabby, too-smart-for-her-own-good female who was giving Ike's heart and life fits.

She wasn't everything that was wrong for him now. She was sleeping. He could love her all he wanted and she wasn't likely to give him a lick of lip.

Pansy stirred, opened an eye and spotted him. She should have given a noisy howl of greeting and demanded a solid ten of petting and rubbing before going outside. Instead, the damned dog just put her head back down at Ginger's feet.

Contrary females seemed to stick together.

He was just about to push off his shoes, crash on the couch and just plain watch her for a while…when his private cell phone did a song and dance. He punched it fast, hoping the sound wouldn't wake Ginger, and hustled toward the kitchen, where she wasn't likely to overhear voices.

"It's me," the caller announced...which meant it was Tucker. Two weeks rarely passed without his older brother checking in, but that was before he'd gotten married.

"I hope you're not going to give me an extensive report on the honeymoon," Ike said. "I'm too young for those kinds of details."

"Hey, I gave you the birds and bees talk when you were nine, didn't I? If I recall, you threatened to throw up. You said the whole thing sounded gross and like nothing you'd ever do."

"Sometimes I think it's a good thing the parents were never home," Ike said wryly. "I'm pretty sure their lecture on sex would have been a lot more tame. But in the meantime...is your new wife leaving you for me yet? And how are the boys?"

"The boys are why I'm calling." Tucker already had a ten-year-old and had inherited an extra ten-year-old boy with his marriage. "I was wondering if you could take them on this weekend. Not the whole weekend. Just Saturday and Saturday night."

"You just got home from a honeymoon and now you already need more free time together?"

"Something like that. She has to do a thing with her parents. Her parents are, shall we say, challenging. If I go with her, it'll be better. But the boys would be bored beyond sanity— we could drag them, but…" Tucker suddenly paused. "Uh-oh."

"Uh-oh what?"

"You usually jump at the chance to corrupt my kid. The chance to corrupt two—and spend the night on Whisper Mountain—would usually get a fast yes out of you. So…something new going on in your private life? Don't worry about the boys, I can—"

"Of course I'll take the boys."

"There's only one little extra problem…"

"What?"

"A couple of kittens. It's pretty obvious to me that cats can stay alone for twenty-four hours, but the boys ganged up on me, claimed they're too little, the kittens have to come with the deal."

"You know I have to bring Pansy. And that Pansy is deathly afraid of cats."

"Your dog is deathly afraid of everything. Still. It's because I raised such a smart younger brother that I knew you'd be able to figure it out. Maybe the girl in your life could come along."

"What girl?"

"The one you haven't told me about. I can't believe it. Which one of the two hundred single women bringing you casseroles and pecan pies finally wrangled you into a date?"

"None of them."

"I should have guessed you'd have to import.

Even in high school, you liked a hot pepper a whole lot more than you went for sugar."

"That's the most ridiculous thing I've ever heard." He suffered Tucker's hounding him a little longer, without telling him about Ginger, at least nothing more than he'd told his sister. Considering how tight the siblings had always been, he wasn't sure why he wasn't in a rush to share everything about her. He had before.

But Ginger wasn't like any woman he'd ever had in his life—or his heart—before. She was more precious. The relationship more precarious. His damn heart too unguarded.

Tucker eventually rang off. When Ike turned around, he found Ginger standing in the doorway. Her feet were bare. She looked as if she'd shoveled her hair, her cheeks had a fresh pinkness, and she was almost smiling.

"I slept like the dead."

"Yeah, it looked like you were out pretty cold."

"For more than three hours, for heaven's sake."

He nodded. "It's the recliner. I swear, it's some kind of narcotic chair. You turn on the TV, sit in the recliner and that's it, instant sleep. It's a guarantee." And man, he thought, she'd needed that serious nap. She looked like herself again, full of perk and spirit.

She lifted her arms, did something with her swarm of hair, clipped it somehow—but she was still eyeing him from the doorway. "It sounded as if you were talking to family?"

"I was. Tucker. Tucker's the oldest, then me, then Rosemary. Tucker just got married a few months ago, turned into one of those blended families—he's got two boys now, age ten. And he wanted me to babysit them over the weekend."

"Of course you said no."

He lifted an eyebrow. "You might as well know now. I never say no to kids."

"I'll be darned. Who'd have thunk it? That you

were a soft touch for kids and dogs and other vulnerable things?"

"I sense an insult in there somewhere."

She grinned, but it was a short one. "I'm going home. My car's still over by the bank, but it's a short walk."

"You need dinner."

"I do," she agreed, "but thanks to you, I really have to get home. I called my grandfather, and as usual, you were right. That's getting annoying, Doc. How often you're right. It's a very unlikable quality in any man. Anyway...Gramps was over the moon about having a great-grandchild. He was immediately charging off to tell Rachel. My grandmother."

Ike winced.

"Yeah, well...he was happy. No question. Never asked me who the father was, which seems a measure of how far his mind has gone. But honestly, I need to go home, see him face to face, see what's what."

"I understand." He did understand. He just didn't want her gone. He hadn't finished grilling her...and they'd left a serious conversation with thorns still sticking his heart. About how there was no "us." About his place in her life.

Or about the place he didn't have in her life.

"If you wanted to be a good boy, you'd drive me to my car. But it really won't kill me to walk three blocks—"

"Of course I'll drive you," he said, only to hear his pager go off.

She chuckled. "I should have expected that. Well, thanks for saving me, handsome." She hiked over, lifted up on tiptoe, brushed her lips across his. It wasn't an ultra long, ultra deep kiss. But it was long enough, deep enough, for her eyes to close, for the sound of a sigh to mingle with tastes and luxurious textures and the sweet, giving shape of her lips. And then she lifted her head.

She'd called him *handsome*. And she'd kissed

him like a dream. And she smiled at him now with pure mischief.

And then she left.

He had to answer his pager. He had to let Pansy out for a serious walk. But for a moment he just stood there, thinking he was never going to survive a relationship with that woman. No way, no how. She messed with his head. There was no rest with her around.

The whole peaceful, stressless life he'd carved out so carefully—gone in a *pffft*. The minute he met her. And it was only getting worse.

When Ginger pulled into the drive, she immediately aimed for the kitchen. Earlier that day, she'd left cash and a vase of garden flowers for Sarah. Sara had taken the flowers, left the money and made some kind of cheesy-crusted chicken and a platter of roasted root vegetables. The baking pans were still sitting on the counter, so the boys must have already eaten. She heaped up a plate, grabbed silverware and carried the dinner with her as she searched for Gramps.

The evening was too cool to sit on the porch, so she figured he must be near the TV. Not. She checked his room, the library, the backyard, the bathroom. Still no Gramps. Worried now, she climbed the stairs to the second story...and finally picked up the vague murmur of conversation coming from a distance.

The open door to the attic would have been a telling clue, if she'd had reason to believe— in a hundred zillion years—that Gramps could conceivably have climbed all the way from the ground floor to the attic.

"What are you two doing up here?" She was still carrying her plate, but it was mostly empty now. She set it on a dusty crate, narrowed her eyes at the boys. Both Cornelius and Gramps were settled in rocking chairs, talking like kids in a sandbox. Both rockers had spokes or parts of the seat missing, and likely a generation of dust on top.

"Sweetheart! I'm so glad you're home!" Gramps didn't rise from the chair or even try, just bent forward to accept her greeting kiss and hug.

"I've been looking all over for you two. What possessed you to climb all those stairs?"

"Well, I admit we're tuckered." Cornelius spoke up first. "But Cashner here was all excited at dinner. He recalled there used to be some things in the attic here—"

"A crib. A toy chest. A wicker basket. I didn't know what all, but I knew there was a heap of old baby things up here. And we found them. But then we both got tired after all the climbing and decided we'd sit a spell."

She turned around. Saw. The attic was lit by skylights and two hanging bald lightbulbs. In midsummer, a massive attic fan helped chase off the heat, but at this time of year, the space was

just stifling and dusty. Ginger remembered fear-
ing all the bogeymen up here—the ones waiting
to come get her if she dared go to sleep.

There were no nightmares up here now—
just generations of Gautier stuff that no one
could seem to throw away. Suitcases and hope
chests and steamer trunks. Antique clocks that
didn't run, a Jenny Lind couch missing spokes,
lamps missing shades. Every which way Ginger
glanced, there was more.

And abruptly she spotted the bedraggled
guitar case. It was her grandmother's old Gibson.
Ginger hadn't seen it since she was a little girl.
She crouched down to open it—when Gramps
and Cornelius abruptly yanked her back to the
present.

"Rachel! Come look at these things and see
if you can think there's anything Ginger could
use."

She straightened, turned to face her grandfather. "It's me," she said firmly. "I'm Ginger, Gramps."

"Yes, of course." He looked bewildered for a moment, then resumed his rocking. "Well, Rachel and I were talking earlier, sweetheart. She was thinking that the whole upstairs wing is bigger than the usual house. You and your husband and the baby could redo whatever you wanted, make it into a completely independent apartment if you wanted. There'd be room for the baby. And more babies. And more babies. And then they could grow up with the tea, like Gautiers all do. Be part of the land, their history." Cashner frowned suddenly. "Forgive me, honey, but I can't just this minute remember your husband's name."

Ginger pushed a hand through her hair.

"Well, it doesn't matter what his name is. It'll come to me. Anyhow, what do you think of that idea? Cornelius thinks it's as brilliant as I do."

Cornelius nodded from the far rocking chair,

where he looked darned close to dozing off. She needed to get them downstairs. Separately. Both looked more frail than the heap of tattered lace hanging from a lamp in the far corner.

But as her gaze was drawn in that direction, she spotted the cache of baby things stored under a rafter. The crib was wood, and undoubtedly wouldn't meet today's safety standards, but beneath it was a toy box, painted with puppies and kittens and baby ducklings. Dirty now, but a true treasure. And the jewel of the lot was buried in the corner—a white wicker basket on wheels, with a crown of organza draping the sides.

It would have to be cleaned up, repainted, the old organza ripped off and a new mosquito netting sewn on to replace it…but Ginger touched the basket and felt a sudden clutch in her throat. It was so clearly a bed for a cherished baby princess. Her mom had snoozed in this basket, and her grandmother in the generation before that. It was so easy to imagine another baby in there, napping, all cuddled up, surrounded by all the family love and history and treated like the princess she deserved to be.

Or maybe it'd be a strapping boy this time—it was about time the Gautiers came through with some smart, sturdy boys. The netting might look a little sissy for a boy, unfortunately. But if the basket could just be cleaned and fixed, Ginger could so easily picture pulling the basket wherever she was, from room to room, so that baby would always be with her.

And just like that, she felt a burst of longing so fierce she could hardly breathe. She wanted the baby more than she wanted her own breath.

She pictured Ike. So far the only way she was keeping her head above water—barely above water—was on his charity. The cook. The gardener. The one to gallop in—maybe not on a white horse, but definitely with a bloodhound in tow—whenever she had a problem.

Only he couldn't save her forever.

She had to find a way to rescue herself. She couldn't talk about loving Ike, about being in love with him—not while she was a charity case. He'd been stuck with her because he was a good guy and she sure needed help. But neither of them would survive a relationship that was so one-sided.

She couldn't just take.

She needed to give, as well.

Chapter Ten

Ike finally pulled into his driveway on Sunday evening. He'd had a blast with his nephews on Whisper Mountain. They'd stayed up late, camped in the high mountain cabin, fished, ate junk food, told ghost stories and of course, made huge fires—everything the boys wanted to do. Everything he loved to do with them, as well… although Ginger was never far from his mind.

He'd checked his home phone and office phone and pager at least a dozen times over the weekend. There were messages. But none from Ginger.

He plunked down his gear from the weekend and headed straight for the shower, thinking that a few days of separation had likely been a good idea anyway.

If she didn't think there was an "us"—or any potential of an "us"—after all they'd shared, then just maybe he needed to cool his jets. He wasn't sixteen anymore. And even when he'd been sixteen, he hadn't panted or drooled after a girl who didn't give him a yes signal. Rejection wasn't fun then, and was even less fun now.

But that didn't stop him from thinking about her.

Monday morning, he woke up to a bright, sunny day and a serious case of determination. Mondays he tried to keep free. He'd see any patients who called in, but otherwise, Ruby had the day off and wasn't there to plague him about paperwork and files. He intended to enjoy the day or die trying.

Before nine, he'd stashed a fishing pole, a blanket and a picnic satchel complete with dog food and a water dish for Pansy. He had a plan.

The same plan he always had.

To not live the way his high-powered parents had lived. He and his brother and sister all had the same roughed-up sores from having parents who were wonderful, fantastic, extraordinary people...but who were never there. They were always too busy, too committed, always on call for complicated surgeries. Ike was the only one who'd gone near a medical career, but he'd done it drastically differently from how he'd grown up.

There was always time to put his feet up. To stick a pole in a creek. To take kids on a camping weekend. To crash in a hammock with a book and a beer after a long day.

"You and I understand laziness," he said to

Pansy, who was rarely allowed on the front seat of the truck and was in her glory, riding with the windows down, her best guy next to her. Everything was right in their world. The dog leaned over and smooshed a wet tongue on his cheek.

"I know, I know. You love me. And I love you right back. And we're going to do nothing today. Maybe nap under a cypress tree. Fish a little. Chew on a bone." He glanced at Pansy. "Yeah, I brought you a bone. Made a whole separate trip to the butcher, just for you. But this time, try to remember to chew on it before burying it, okay?"

Pansy, judging from the adoration in her eyes, was willing to follow the entire day's plan without a single howl.

Only something happened. He couldn't explain it, but the truck developed a crazy problem. Instead of aiming south—toward his favorite fishing spot—the darned truck turned east. Ike couldn't believe it.

"What's going on here?" he asked Pansy, who by then had dropped her head to his shoulder and was already on vacation time, snoring between drools and dream snorting sounds.

The truck made another turn. Then another.

"This isn't happening," he told Pansy. "The GPS must be broken. Or the steering column."

Of all the damned…Ike scowled as the Gautier house came into view. For damned sure, he hadn't planned to see her. Or think about her. This entire day was supposed to be a playing-hooky agenda. He didn't want or need another slap in the heart from Miss Gautier.

He muttered a few more aw hells before parking and turning the key. He left the door open for Pansy, who wasn't immediately inclined to get out. Ike's gaze riveted on another vehicle in the driveway. A shiny black convertible. A rental, he could see from the plates.

An indulgent toy, that car. Wasteful. The convertible top rarely useable. Only two seats and no space. How impractical was that in real life?

Ike had always wanted one. They were just so damned…sexy. The immediate question, of course, was whom the car belonged to.

Since three days rarely went by without his checking on Cashner, Ike took brisk, self-righteous steps up the porch to the front door. Knocked, then poked his head inside.

"Just me!" he called out. "Just going in this direction, figured I'd stop by and sponge a mug of tea…"

It was his traditional greeting, and when he paused in the kitchen doorway, he put his hands in the air. In another life, he really could have made it as an actor, no matter what his family said. "Well, darn, I didn't realize you had company. I don't want to interrupt—"

"Nonsense," Cashner said, his response as

predictable as sunshine. "Sit down, sit down. Ginger hid some of my best black teas, said I was overdoing it, but I've got a good green mint brewing. Steve, this is Ike MacKinnon. He's my doctor. And Ike, this is Steve Winters. He's here from Detroit."

"Chicago," the visitor immediately corrected.

"Yeah, I always get those two mixed up. Steve's waiting for Ginger. They worked together up north. Or they were both at the same hospital or something. He's a doctor like you. So I guess I can call you both Doc, and then I don't have to worry if I forget your names, huh?"

Ike got his own mug and poured his own tea— in case the stranger happened to notice that he knew his way around the Gautier place. Still, it took a minute before he could finally sit down and take a serious look at the jerk.

"So…where is Ginger?" he asked amiably.

"She just left a bit ago. Doing a grocery and bank run. I swear she left the drive about the same time Steve drove in. They could have passed each other. But anyways, like I told him, nothing in Sweet Valley is too far a drive. Ginger'll be back before lunch, for sure. I'd think before eleven."

"So you're Cashner's doctor," said the Chicago turd.

"Sure am."

Ginger hadn't said the creep's name was Steve. But the father of her baby was a doctor, and she'd been in Chicago, and now the son of a sea dog showed up here out of the blue, and with that car. Ike didn't need a calculator to add up the clues.

The guy's external appearance alone was beyond offensive. Chinos with a crease. Loafers, the kind of butter-soft leather that had never seen an ounce of dirt or a puddle. A navy-blue polo shirt, short sleeves, the kind that showed off serious upper-body muscle and toned arms. The idiot was tanned.

Ike struggled to find something to like, but

that was sure a tough sled. The guy had a shave so fresh the razor was probably still dripping. Square jaw. A smile that showed off lots of money in orthodontia. Eyes such a cool blue that he probably had contacts. Brown hair. Lots of it. Not straight or curly, just sort of thick and wavy. Had a Dartmouth class ring. Broad shoulders, clean-cut smile. The whole package was tall, lean, smooth. Oh, and cultured.

Talk about a scuzzball.

"You're a long way from your neck of the woods," Ike said. "Or do you have family or friends in this area?"

"No, no. Only one I know is Ginger. But she called me on Saturday night. And after talking to her..." Another of those blinding-white smiles. "Well, I hadn't seen her in a while. I knew she was from here. She often talked about the tea plantation, her grandparents. So..."

"So she's expecting you?" Ike asked, his voice reeking careless interest.

"No, no, it's a surprise. After talking to her… well, I got it in my head that I had to see her. Took a bit to make arrangements—"

"I'm sure it did. You're a surgeon?"

"Yeah, how'd you know?"

"I didn't. Or I guessed from something someone said. That you spent most of your time literally at the hospital, so it was easy to—"

"Yeah. Cardiovascular." He paused, as if making sure the importance of that sunk into Ike. Then he added, "And you're, like, the town doctor here?"

"Yes."

"Get a lot of scraped knees and flu and chicken pox?" Scuzzball smiled genially, as if to make sure Ike understood he was joking.

He wasn't joking. Ike understood full well that they might both be doctors, but in the jerk's view, Ike was low class and Scuzzball ruled the universe. *Maybe* he'd let Ike shine his loafers some day. *That* kind of smile.

Abruptly Ike heard a howl, then a growl of thunder, then the thunder of hooves. Pansy showed up in the doorway, wild-eyed.

"Oh, my God," said God's Gift to Women.

"Yeah, she's a bloodhound. C'mere, girl. It's just a little rain. Nothing to be scared of. And if you broke through Cashner's screen again, I'm gonna have to shoot you."

"She doesn't break through the screen anymore," Cashner said. "Ever since we put that different latch on the door, she can push it down herself, get in on her own."

Pansy, being Pansy, had to smell anything new in her realm, so she abruptly forgot about the storm the instant she spotted Steve. Ike watched the jerk's eyes widen.

Since a response was obviously required of Ike, he immediately said, "No, no, Pansy."

Pansy responded to serious commands—at least most of the time. Well, some of the time. In this case, she was too busy to listen and put out her big old wet, drooling muzzle and sniffed up Steve from ankle to knee to leg and—almost— to crotch.

"Oh, my God," Steve said again.

"Aw, man. I'm so sorry." Ike slowly stood up. "Pansy. Go lie down. How could you do that to a visitor? Hey, I'll take care of it." He ambled toward the sink, soaked a dish towel, brought the sopping cloth back. "It does dry. Won't look so much like snot when it's dry—"

"I'll do it." The perfect smile slipped. Suddenly there was a little acid in the eyes, a narrowed look, as if Scuzzball was starting to realize he wasn't exactly among friends.

Outside, there was a sudden burst of noise and commotion. A car door slammed. Pansy started a joyous howl and tail thump. Cornelius's voice mingled with the sound of Ginger's laughter. They seemed to be arguing about who was carrying in the grocery bags—and both of them were winning.

The commotion only took a few seconds—but long enough for Ike to figure out something he didn't want to figure out. If Scuzzball was here, after a phone call with Ginger, then she'd likely told him about the pregnancy. And if he responded by showing up, it didn't sound likely that he thought his relationship with Ginger was over and done with.

Ginger charged through the back door, carrying a couple of light sacks, and almost fell when Pansy rushed to greet her. Cornelius, just behind her, carted an overflowing grocery sack that appeared to be splitting. A ball of lettuce fell, bounced on the floor. Then a small bag of oranges.

Ginger was still laughing, but she seemed to forget the groceries altogether when she looked up. Her eyes went soft. "Ike," she said, and probably would have said something more—until she glanced around the table and recognized Scuzzball. She did a double take. "Steve? Why on earth are you here?"

"We needed to talk."

"We did talk."

"On the phone. I knew we needed to talk face-to-face."

The minute she put down the two sacks, her hand flew to her stomach in a protective gesture. "Maybe we do. But I wish you had called before showing up here."

"Honey," Cashner said, "I think you're not being very welcoming, especially when someone's come all this way to see you."

Ike blanked out most of that awkward chitchat while he debated his options.

He could knock the guy's block off. For sure, that was his favorite choice. He'd never had much violence in him, but for Scuzzball, he could manage some serious steam.

A second option was to stay quiet, but maneuver himself carefully between Ginger and the jerk. Just to make sure nothing happened that she didn't want. To protect her. Or to tell Pansy to attack, if all else failed. Pansy wouldn't have a clue what that meant, but the jerk would be distracted.

Ike liked all those options. Except for the one option he really, really didn't want to do.

Ike didn't sigh, didn't kick a chair, didn't do anything to indicate that he was not happy. "You know what?" he asked, in a loud enough voice to garner attention. "Cashner and I are going for a little drive. Maybe get some lunch. We'll be back here, say, in an hour and a half. Max."

He wanted to look at Ginger. He wanted to talk to her, wanted just a few minutes—even one minute, one short minute—before he left her alone with the bozo. He could even feel her eyes on his back…but nothing he wanted seemed remotely relevant just then.

It took energy and persuasion to get Cashner to his feet, to steer him from the kitchen, find a light jacket for him, find his shoes, get him outside and into the truck. There was a light rain falling by then. Cashner was not of an age to be comfortable climbing in and out of a truck. And then there was Pansy.

Pansy, of course, wanted to go with them. Pansy couldn't imagine Ike leaving in the truck without her. But handling both Pansy and Cashner in the front seat was impossible, besides which he wanted her with Ginger.

Pansy gave him The Eyes—the desolate, abandoned, sad eyes—when he told her to stay.

Somehow by the time he started the truck engine, he felt as if he'd run a marathon. Dark clouds scuttled in front of the sun, changing an overcast day into an ominously gloomy one. Cashner didn't care. Once he finally settled himself in the truck, he was all about an outing. Happy as a clam, he said in a conspiratorial whisper, "Did you know Rachel and I are going to have a baby? Can you believe it? She's over the moon!"

Oh, man. It was going to be a long hour and a half.

Talk about feeling deserted. Cornelius peeled out the back door almost as fast as Ike hauled Gramps out the front. She was stuck not only with Steve in the kitchen, but a disconsolate hound trailing every move she made—and sacks of groceries to put away, most of which were perishable.

"I still don't understand why you're here," she repeated. She stashed milk, butter, cheese and eggs in the fridge, then closed the door to face him again.

He was just as good-looking as he'd always been. He had the same intelligence and perception in his eyes—qualities that made him an outstanding surgeon. It was just a shame he didn't have as much perception and intelligence in his character. He didn't look ill at ease now. He never looked ill at ease. Steve could walk into any place, any group, and never fear he couldn't handle himself.

"Did you think," he asked, "that you could just call, tell me you were pregnant and think I'd have nothing to say after that?"

Ah. One of his best tricks. Putting her on the defensive. "I absolutely expected to hear from you. But not yet, and not here. I know my telling you about the pregnancy had to be a serious shock. And I assumed you'd want time to think. Not that you'd suddenly show up here."

The next grocery bag held freezer stuff. Peppermint-stick ice cream. Peach-and-cream frozen yogurt. Blueberry-swizzle ice cream. Double vanilla.

This past week, she'd somehow wanted ice cream with every meal. Even breakfast.

Since Steve didn't immediately comment, she filled up the freezer, then turned around, looked at him and zoomed straight to the counter for a mug of fresh tea. "It was all right with what's-her-name that you came down here?" she asked.

"Audrey. We broke up." Steve hadn't budged from his chosen seat at the head of the table. His gaze tracked her as relentlessly as Pansy did. "I missed you."

Okay. So this meeting never had much potential to go well, but now she was pretty sure it was going down ugly. She sat at the far end of the table with one hand on her mug of tea and the other on Pansy...who finally quieted once she could lean against Ginger.

"Nothing was the same after you left," he said with the same searing look in his eyes that she'd once taken for sincerity. "I was more or less pushed into that engagement. It was a joining of families, schools and ties we'd both had forever. It wasn't about feeling anything for her, the way I did for you. The way I still do feel for you."

It was all she could do to not toss the hot tea on his head. To not give him a good piece of her mind, including expletives and swear words and a good loud tongue-lashing. She'd always let loose when she was angry or upset.

But this time…well, this time was just different. She couldn't put rain back in a rain cloud. The milk had already spilled, the egg had cracked and all those other metaphors. She wasn't angry with him anymore—which was a strangely reassuring realization.

He just didn't matter enough to waste her temper on. Steve, though, seemed encouraged that she wasn't giving him more lip. "Having a child together changes everything. I always thought we had a lot going for us—until I messed it up. I know I hurt you. And I'm sorry. I know it'll take time for you to forgive me, to trust me again, but—"

"Hold it." Not expressing her temper was one thing. Listening to his drivel was another. "This child is yours. I expect support from you. And I expect to listen if and when you put out a plan to be part of the child's life. But those aren't issues for today. We don't need to talk about those things for quite a while."

"I want—"

"I don't much care what you want," she said pleasantly.

"Love doesn't just die, Ginger—"

"Oh, yeah, it does. The man I fell in love with didn't exist. I saw qualities in you, character in you, that weren't real. You're smart. You're a brilliant surgeon. There are lots of reasons why a child with your genes has every chance to turn into a terrific human being. But to love or trust you again? Never. You'll cheat the first chance you get. No matter who you marry."

"That's not fair."

"I'm not interested in fair. I'm not interested in having any more conversations with you. The only tough thing for me was deciding whether to call you and let you know about the pregnancy. I decided I had to. That you had the right to know. But I'll never have a relationship again with you, Steve."

"We were good together," he began.

"We had pretty good sex—when it conveniently fit into your busy schedule. At the time, it never occurred to me that everything we did revolved around your needs, what you wanted—but you don't have to hit me over the head with a bat twice. I got it."

"Losing you changed me. Changed how I thought about love and what I wanted in my life."

She refrained from a noisy, inelegant snort. But barely. "Are you losing your hearing? I don't care."

Some of that rotten character he kept hidden so well finally showed through. "You think I'm going to pay child support without any say in the child's upbringing? You'd better think again. I could sue you for full custody and get it."

She glanced down. "Pansy, did you smell a threat in the air? Or was that just gas?"

"You're not funny."

"Go home, Steve. We can have many civil conversations in the years ahead about the baby. But there's nothing pleasant either of us has to say to each other today."

The charm, the coaxing and endearing expression on his face that she knew so well, slipped off. His eyes turned glacier. "I have more financial resources than you could in a lifetime, and more connections than you could ever dream of. If I want custody of the child, Ginger, don't doubt for a minute that I can get it."

She'd been holding her own, feeling sure of herself until then. Nothing exactly changed. She'd figured out that he was a rat before this. But it still hurt…that someone she'd cared for had such an ugly side. That she hadn't seen it before this. That she'd given freely of herself to someone who could turn around and treat her like dirt.

Maybe it was a crazy moment to realize she'd fallen in love with Ike.

The current mountain of trouble on her head... she'd never really doubted that she could claw her way to the top of it. She was strong. She'd always stood up on her own two feet. She'd never wanted to ask a man into her life out of need.

But once all the trouble was sorted out—if that wildly crazy magic was still there with Ike— well then, she was likely to go after him with all she had.

She hadn't known that was the plan, the goal, her heart's dream...until she lost it.

Steve had put her down in a way that she'd never thought she could be put down. She'd chosen once upon a time to give her heart to him, a man with this much venom in him. A man with no respect for her, or respect for what she'd given him.

A man who made her feel small.

She felt like a flower that suddenly closed up tight to protect against frost.

Chapter Eleven

When Ike brought Cashner home, the first thing he noticed was that the black Eclipse was nowhere in sight. That wasn't absolute proof the jerk was gone, but it seemed a good sign.

He pulled up next to the porch, making it easier for Cashner to negotiate the path from his truck to the door, and then hustled around to the passenger side to help him out.

"I want to check your blood pressure before going home," he told Cashner.

"You just want to see my granddaughter. And get your dog."

"Right on both counts, but we're still going to do the BP."

"You're a pain, Ike. I don't know why I like you," Cashner grumbled, but his cheeks were pink. The fresh air and outing had done him good.

He stumbled getting out, but Ike was right there, and Cashner regained his balance almost immediately. Ike glanced around, not exactly looking for Ginger, but definitely expecting Pansy to give out a howl of a hello.

Nothing. Nada. Not a sound. Once inside, he settled Cashner in a kitchen chair to check his pulse and blood pressure. Both numbers were good. Cashner wasn't a spring chicken, but the only thing really wrong with him was a fading mind.

"I think I'm going to hole up for a little rest, Ike."

"Good idea. I'll track down Pansy, and then we'll be on our way. You're doing great. Let's do another outing like that soon."

"You bet."

Cashner was already yawning as he waved a goodbye and ambled toward his room. Ike did a swift pivot, trying to figure out from the clues in the kitchen where Ginger was. A single sandwich plate sat on the counter, an opened bag of Oreos next to it. A water dish sat on the floor—with a place mat under it, forcing Ike to chuckle in spite of himself. His dog wasn't exactly a tidy drinker, but he'd never thought of using a place mat to control the slobber.

Ginger knew his dog. And his dog loved Ginger. But no clues he'd seen so far were enough.

He hiked through the dining room, the hall, poked his head in the living room. It wasn't as if he was worried about either one of them. He just wanted to find Ginger, preferably in the next three seconds. He needed to know how the pow-wow with her ex had gone. He wanted to know if Mr. Flake needed to be tracked down and given the punch in the jaw Ike had been playing and replaying in his head. He wanted to know if she was okay.

Only by accident did he glance out a side window in the back hall. An old-fashioned hammock was tied between two tree limbs, swaying in a winsome breeze. It wasn't hammock weather. It was jacket weather—and it had been damp this morning besides. But there was a foot hanging out of the hammock, with some kind of shoe that tied in a bow.

And below the hammock was his dog. Pansy was sleeping, which was nothing unusual. But she seemed to be sleeping with—almost—her entire head in an empty ice cream container.

No wonder the dog hadn't roused when he got here. Pansy always had her priorities straight. Ice cream came above all else.

He slipped outside, down the step, past the magnolia tree to the two oaks. This wasn't the first time a hammock had been tied between the two trees—the hammock looked almost as old as they did. He crouched down to stroke Pansy's head, which motivated the dog to immediately roll over to demand a tummy massage.

Ike had an eye-level view of Ginger from that angle. She'd put a red blanket under her, zipped up an old white fleece jacket, brought out a poofy pillow for her head and pulled a light blue blanket over her. The foot sticking out was clad in an old-fashioned sneaker, a crazy green-and-yellow plaid with a bow for a fastener. She had a little foot. A delicate ankle. And in spite of the mounded blankets, she looked no bigger than two bits.

His gaze wandered up...the humid air had made her hair curl up, making him think of a cinnamon-colored steel wool after being hit by lightning. Her face, skin that bruised far too easily, was lighter than cream and that soft mouth was beyond-temptation kissable…at least it was for two seconds. But then he realized she'd opened her eyes.

"No," she said.

"Why are you saying no? I didn't ask you a question."

"I'm just saying no, this isn't fair. I am very, very tired of you always seeing me at my worst."

He cocked his head. "You don't seem your worst to me. In fact, you're looking pretty darned edible."

A vulnerable flush climbed her cheeks, but she was still sending out a Ginger scowl. "I meant your stopping by when Steve was here this morning. Your taking Gramps out so he wouldn't hear an argument. Your saving me. Your thinking I needed saving. Your coming through."

"Damn. I can sure see why you'd be annoyed at me for that. Did you have a good nap?" He had to try changing the subject, since his being a nice guy and a good friend seemed to temporarily disgust her.

"A great nap."

"I always sleep great after having ice cream, too. Who had more of that half gallon, you or Pansy?"

"We didn't eat a whole half gallon! There was only a third of a gallon in there! And we both needed ice cream. It was a stressful morning."

"I hope it was even more stressful for your visitor." He added genially, "I was glad to get a look at him. Helped me get an idea what kind of guy appealed to you."

She pulled the blanket over her head. "Go away. I don't want to talk to you any more today."

He tugged on the blanket, then gave the edge to Pansy, who was more than willing, always, to take a length of blanket and run with it. Once the thief had her loot, she sank yet again on the ground to snooze, leaving Ginger blanketless—

although she still had on the white fleece jacket
and old chinos. And those shoes.

"You know who Steve reminded me of?" he
asked.

"I'm afraid you're going to tell me."

"My parents."

"Say what?" She started to sit up, with the obvious intention of getting out of the hammock,
but when Ike saw the empty space, he plopped
down next to her.

The hammock temporarily rocked precari-
ously—there was a serious risk of both of them
being dumped on the ground—but eventually
it settled down. As far as Ike was concerned,
his settling next to her was an ideal position,
because their hips and shoulders were glued.
A fair number of her body parts were trapped
against him, just as a fair number of his were
against her.

Life was good.

She shot him a look. Okay, so they wer

exactly all that comfortable. But he was next to her. For a few minutes he needed her attention. So having her snuggled against him was still a bonus.

"I know I already mentioned that my parents are both surgeons. If you met them, I know you'd like them. They're not just brilliant at what they do, but they're devoted to their patients, to saving lives. They make no end of sacrifices to save those lives."

She squirmed once, trying to find a less glued-on-him position, but really, the hammock had them trapped close. She lifted her head. "This may amaze you, but I don't have a clue what your parents have to do with Steve, other than they're all in the medical profession."

"But it's what first drew you, I'm guessing. That he was a great doctor. The kind of person who sacrificed to save lives. And who does save ~ves, doesn't just talk about it."

Well..." She hesitated. "Yes, you're right. I

did admire him. Some doctors get a frosty reputation with other hospital staff, but Steve was
decent to everyone. No temper tantrums. No
arrogance on the surface. No God complex that
anyone saw."

"I think," Ike said carefully, "that high-powered people, driven people, the really seriously
high-achiever people…just have some things in
common."

"Like?"

"Well, you can't say a doctor's selfish when he
sacrifices so much for his patients and gives up
so much of his personal time. But that skill be-
comes more important than anything else. More
important than a spouse or kids or anyone else
in their personal lives. Maybe…" He hesitated.
"Maybe there's some glory in being so special,
so different from so-called normal people. I
don't know. But I do know they expected other
people to cater to their needs."

He waited.

And waited some more.

She'd given up battling for distance, and instead, just leaned her head against his shoulder and gave in to the closeness. He couldn't see her expression, but she was listening.

"Well, that was very like Steve," she said finally. "The glory thing. If he was in a hurry, he expected others to get out of the way. If he was a no-show, he expected others to understand. It didn't seem egotistical to me...until I finally realized that's how it always was. His life was more important than anyone else's." She added wryly, "I thought you'd be pretty disgusted by the four-hundred-dollar loafers and no socks."

"What? You think I'm that superficial that I'd give a damn what the guy looked like?"

"No, no," she said immediately.

It's not like he'd ever admit that Scuzzball's whole look—and good looks—had given him a heart attack. Ike didn't give a damn about appearance issues like that. But if they mattered to

Ginger, well, it wouldn't have been a good sign. "So," he said, "somehow I suspect he showed up to talk you into going back with him."

"He did."

"Since he didn't call you first, he must have been afraid you'd say no. He thought he was more likely to persuade you, if he saw you in person."

She hesitated, but then her response was quick enough. "Yup. You're getting all the square pegs in the square holes."

"And…then what happened?"

"In a nutshell…I said no, I wasn't going back with him. He insulted me. I told him to leave. He threatened me. I lost my temper." She shrugged. "Just your everyday melodrama."

She apparently wanted him to see the humor in it…but he didn't. It just seemed like one more traumatic thing thrown at Ginger when she'd had a nonstop heap of them in the last month. "So… I'm guessing the subject of the baby came up?"

"Oh, yeah. Which, I have to admit, threw me. Obviously he was unsettled when I first called and told him. But I just assumed there was no reason to have another conversation until after we both had time to consider all the implications. Instead...well, it didn't take long for him to go on the attack. I mean...I told him upfront that he had a legal right to be part of the child's life. But instead of being nice back, he seemed to get more angry. He threatened to sue me for total custody."

Ike had another mental picture of himself punching out the jerk. But he kept his voice even, not wanting Ginger to stop talking. "What happened after that?"

"That was pretty much the end of it. He left, and Pansy and I galloped straight for the ice cream."

She fell silent after that. He wanted to know more, but she'd answered the one killing issue that had been rug-burning his nerves. She was over the hotshot doc. Maybe the breakup had been fairly recent, but Ike hadn't heard a hint of warmth in her voice, seen any in her eyes.

And since she'd gone limp on his chest, he relaxed, too, just let the hammock sway in a slow, lazy rock. The sun tipped past a cloud, warmed their heads in spite of the damp chill in the air. A bare breeze ruffled the grass, sifted the scents of wet leaves and somewhere, a brush pile burning. A dog barked in the distance, not loud enough to wake Pansy, just a canine greeting its owner from some other property down the road.

"Ike?"

"Hmm?"

"I don't want to say anything about your parents, because I've never met them. Or any more about Steve, because I've had more than enough of talking about him. But…" She hesitated. "I can see the other side of the fence. People who have the gift and the skill to save lives, to stand up for people who can't help themselves…that's a great thing, not a bad thing. But it also makes them different, whether they want to be or not."

"So what's your point?"

She put a palm on his chest. "The point isn't about my ex-guy or your parents. It's about you. You have those same issues. Your pager is always on. That's who you are. It's a good quality. Not a bad one."

"I'm *nothing* like them. I'd never put my job over a spouse or kids."

"Yeah? Well, I've been with you these last few weeks. When the pager makes noise, you're on your feet in two shakes. You go. You don't think twice. You don't need to. It's just who you are."

"Ginger. It's not the same thing. I'm a low achiever, not a driven type in any way."

"Uh-huh."

"Hey. My exam rooms don't have clocks. I wear sandals in the office. The dog goes with me on house calls. Does that sound like someone with a high-stress gene?"

She made a sound. He had a bad feeling it was a chuckle. "Ike, I don't care whether you wear wing tips or sandals. You still run when someone needs you. You're dedicated and you're driven. That's just the way it is."

The hammock quit rocking. "You know, you can be really annoying," he mentioned.

Instead of taking offense, she leaned forward and looked at him with an amused expression. "That's the real problem, isn't it? Because even when you're annoyed…like now…you still want to kiss me."

"More than kiss you," he immediately corrected her.

Out of nowhere, she turned into an estrogen grenade. "Damn it, Ike! Did it never occur to you that that's what I want, too? Only there's a huge difference between what I want and what I can have! And you're just making it harder!"

She took off from the hammock and stomped to the house, going out of her way to let the screen door slam behind her. He stared after her, dumbfounded.

He was the one who should be mad, not her. He was the one who'd been offended, not her. It bit like a steel trap that she'd compared him to Scuzzball Steve…and, for that matter, to his parents.

"Pansy. Go truck." He didn't snarl, because he never snarled at his dog, but the dark, snarly mood followed him the whole rest of the week.

Ginger thought he was *driven?* That he wore the "dedicated" halo that her egotistical ex did? Not. Never. He'd been called to medicine, yeah, but he didn't have a driven bone in his body, and had done everything but stand on his head to avoid a pressure-cooker practice.

His parents valued their reputations, their status. For damn sure, Dumbo Steve did.

Not him. It hurt. That Ginger didn't know him better than that by now. And all week, he made a point of choosing attire that reflected his true personality. Frayed chinos. Shirts dug out of the back of his closet, the ones where you could see threads in the collar—if anyone looked, but why would they? They were soft as butter, old friends, still had plenty of wear in them.

He saved on shaving cream for seven whole days, too.

He saw Ginger all week, because that's how it was in a small town. You had to be careful about having a fight, because you couldn't avoid running into anyone for long—like at the bank window, in line at the grocery store, driving into a gas station just as she finished filling her gas tank.

They waved.

He fumed. He'd get around to talking to her again. As soon as he figured out what to say— and really, that wasn't particularly tough. It was true, he carried a pager.

True, he lived with interruptions all the time. But in his heart, his life, he believed that family came first. If a patient was in a car accident, yeah, he'd let that interrupt breakfast. But if someone he loved needed him, then that mattered more than a patient calling for allergy medicine. It was about balance. The balance his parents never had. The balance her ex wouldn't understand if it bit him in the butt.

By the following Tuesday, Ike had finally simmered down. He even let a few of her comments leak through his rock head. She'd admitted wanting him. She'd just said she couldn't have what she wanted.

How come he hadn't remembered she'd said that before? That he could handle. Midmorning Tuesday, between patients, he put in a quick call to Sarah.

She answered, sounding crabby and tired— the way she always did. "How're the kids?" he asked first.

"They're for sale. The youngest is cheapest. But you can name your price."

He laughed. "That little squirt's my favorite, you know. I take it you're having a time-out kind of morning?"

"Yeah. I used to give a time-out to the kids. Now I give myself a time-out, sit on the porch with a cup of coffee, let them tear up the house while I get a break."

"Good thinking." He cleared his throat. "Sarah, I called because I need to ask you a favor."

"You know I owe you the moon. Whatever it is, it's a yes."

"Well, I have an idea. But to make it work, I need someone—not me—to gang up on Ginger. Would you be willing to bully her for a good cause? Seriously ruffle her feathers?"

"Are you kidding, Doc? That'll probably be the most fun I'll have this week."

That was exactly what Ike hoped she'd say. And for the first time since the quarrel with Ginger, he felt his spirits lift. Not soar, but lift.

You couldn't win a war—or woo a woman—

without weapons. He'd forgotten what a fighter she was. But then, maybe she didn't realize that he was a fighter himself—especially when it came to someone he loved.

Ginger thought she heard the back door slam, but Gramps and Cornelius were at the senior center for the whole morning. She'd used the promise of quiet to turn the dining room into a temporary office. The house had two offices and a library, all of which had desks, but none with a space as big as the dining room table.

Since that dreadful morning with Ike, she'd buried herself in paper, all tidily organized in heaps. There were piles of tax records, expense records and agricultural resources on tea. The next group had lists of historical buyers. Tea tasters. (Who knew there was a degree in tea tasting from certain universities?) Then came the corral of folders. A folder for investment strategies, another for monthly spreadsheets, cost basis, market graphs, profit and loss projections.

At the moment, she was pretty close to crying—not because she was overwhelmed. She'd worked in hospital administration, so she knew how to develop projections and put a plan together. It was just that the dynamics of an agricultural enterprise were worlds different from a hospital setup.

Besides which, she needed to know everything all at once.

She had a clear goal, had figured it out the morning they'd argued. There was no thinking about Ike until her life crises were fixed—which meant that she needed to create a business plan to take to the bank. She needed a presentation that would knock Lydia Trellace's socks off. She needed the numbers to be true, the ideas defensible—a plan that she could defend up one side and down the other.

And she'd been studying all these files of information for days. She just didn't have a plan together yet.

A thud and a swear word in the kitchen made her jerk her head up. A clatter of pans followed.

"Who's there?" Ginger rose to her feet in a scatter of paper.

"Who do you think's here? How many people do you have cooking in your kitchen, anyway?"

Ginger immediately relaxed. She'd have known Sarah's surly voice anywhere, even if she rarely saw the woman. She searched through the heaps of paper on the dining room table, found one of her empty teacups and carted it into the kitchen.

Sarah glanced up, but continued banging and clattering and slamming.

"I've wanted to tell you for ages how much I appreciate your cooking. You're so good. I've loved everything. So has my grandfather."

"Huh. No surprise there. I told you I could cook."

"Um…smells good in here already."

"Not likely. I haven't opened a single package yet."

It was like trying to talk to a porcupine. Yet Ginger liked her…possibly because she could be a wee bit like a porcupine herself sometimes. "I've been leaving you fresh flowers from the garden and some cash. Somehow you always leave the cash."

"Should be obvious. I'm no one's charity case. And I'm paying off my debt to the doc. I didn't ask for anything more than that." Sarah shot her a look.

It was the only look she ever gave her. Annoyed. Roll the eyes, couldn't believe how stupid others were in the universe, generically disgusted. Today she was wearing dark gray twills and a steel-gray sweater. The clothes washed out her face, but they certainly suited her personality.

Then she turned around, and started slamming things on the counter—including a menacingly sized knife. "Could be," she said spritely, "that I thought it was about time someone told you a thing or two. Since you appear to be dumb as a rock, bless your heart."

Ginger blinked. "Um, you're offering me advice?"

"Advice you shouldn't need." Sarah took some round steak from the refrigerator and started beating it with a mallet. It seemed an ideal occupation for her. "Way I hear it, you got to do something about the farm. Got to do something about your grandpa. Got to do something about the young 'un in your belly. And you got Amos Hawthorne in a snit, which seems something you're unusually good at. So…"

"So?"

"So, where were you raised, girl? You're in South Carolina. When you want Southerners to do something, you feed 'em. That's how it's done. How it was always done. How it always will be done."

"You mean like…have a party?" Ginger couldn't fathom the idea—much less the cost of feeding a large number of people.

"I don't mean an ordinary party. I mean a *tea* party. Don't you know nothing about your own upbringing? You treat people like dirt, they act like dirt. You treat people like you care about them, they care back. Can't very well be mean to you if you put on all your manners and Southern charm for them." Sarah stopped pounding. "Assuming you have charm. I haven't seen any of it, myself."

Ginger was thinking. "It's not a bad idea. But honestly, I don't see how I could afford to…"

Sarah snorted. Finished pounding the round steak, and started cutting up potatoes as she'd had experience with a machete in a war. "I know you're a college girl, so I try to forgive your ignorance sometimes, but I swear it's a challenge. Everything isn't about money. You do the tea. Jed, now, his wife makes the best lemon meringue pie you ever ate. The Feinsteins that run the deli, they can make finger sandwiches to die for. Not free. Not them, they wouldn't do nothing for free. But you could think of something you could do in trade—like stock their restaurant with your best teas for a while. And then there's Ruby."

"You mean Ike's Ruby?"

"I know. She dresses a little floozylike. All that color and makeup. But honey, she could straighten out the Middle East if anyone ever had the brains to give her the job. You got all those fancy teapots and containers all over the house. You could put on a party like no one's ever seen. Ruby'd know how to do the decorations, the invitations, how things should look. You'd just have to ask her."

Ginger kept thinking she already had too much on her plate without adding another responsibility. "I love the idea. I really do. People have been great to our family over the years, and just as wonderful since I've come home. But...I can't see how to throw a party just to ask people for help, or for money—"

"Thank the Lord your grandmother never heard you say that." Sarah put butter in a huge cast-iron frying pan, waited until the butter was spitting hot, then dumped in the potatoes with the same violence with which she did everything else. "You don't ask for anything at the party. You never mention money. You just do the party and be a hostess. They'll be waiting for you to ask for money, because they know you need it. But you don't. You just smile and make 'em feel welcome and be gracious."

"Gracious," Ginger echoed.

"You don't have more than a bump, but I'd still go buy a maternity top, because you'll look more helpless. This isn't a time to look strong. This is a time to look delicate. You buy it in a color that's light and soft. You know. Something that's nothing like you. Something a sweet woman might wear."

Ginger leaned an elbow on a counter. "Is it some kind of challenge for you? To insult me every few minutes?"

"Challenge? It's no challenge. You're as easy to insult as anybody I ever met. Course, I don't enjoy insulting just anybody."

Ginger got it. That Sarah was giving her a compliment—an exceptionally back-door compliment—but an expression of friendship nonetheless. She shook her head. "Would you mind my giving you a hug?"

Sarah recoiled. "I got work to do here. Kids waiting for me at home. No time for any more talking."

"Okay, okay. I'm going back to work, too. But…if you want to bring your kids with you, I just want to say they'd be welcome here. Lots of yard to run around in. A lot of steps to run up and down and make a lot of noise. Wouldn't bother anyone here."

Sarah responded with an impatient, "Hmmph." Ginger figured that was the nicest thing she'd said so far in the whole discussion, and headed back to the dining room and her business headaches.

But Sarah's tea party idea hung in her mind, took frame and shape until she couldn't let it go. It was a good idea. Her first instinct was to run it by Ike…but she quelled that impulse.

Ike had helped her more than enough.

Chapter Twelve

Two afternoons later, when Ike pulled into the Gautier driveway, he told himself he'd waited as long as he possibly could. He never failed to check on Cashner less than twice a week. And Sarah had related how Ginger had bought the tea party idea, so naturally he wanted to see how the plans were coming along.

Besides—if he waited any longer to see her, he was likely to go out of his mind.

Above him, a pitiful excuse for a sun had finally shown up—he wasn't complaining. In the rainy season any sun was better than none. Still, it was cool as he hiked up the porch steps, did his brisk double rap on the front door, and poked his head in. "It's just me. Ike. Checking in."

The time was going on four. He'd wanted to come earlier, but a young man with a bad burn had taken a major bite from the afternoon.

Cashner called out a greeting from his bedroom in the back, where Ike found the boys sipping sweet tea and swearing over a canasta game. The small bedroom TV had a court show on, but both men could talk over it. "It's a horrible thing when a grown man has to hide in his bedroom. We've lost control of the house, Ike. The shame is almost more than either of us can handle."

"Oh, the pitiful goings-on around here." Cornelius picked up the song, accidentally filching a card from the pile as Ike pulled out his blood pressure kit.

"What's so terrible?" Ike said nothing about

the cheating. They both did it, every game; it seemed to be their favorite part of playing together.

"It's all about the party next week on Tuesday. Ginger's got the whole household in an uproar."

"What party?" Ike asked in his most innocent voice.

"The *big* party. I think I first heard it was a tea party, but then I heard it was potluck. Doesn't matter to either of us what it is. The problem is, she's cleaning everything. It's not normal. If you sit down anywhere, she'll be scrubbing you with bleach or assaulting you with a vacuum. It's a bad thing when a man can't find peace in his own house. And she wants me to wear a bow tie."

"Oh, no. Not that."

Cashner whispered, "She's having more fun than I've seen her in a long while. Not the worst thing, having to dress up. But don't tell her I said so."

He checked Cashner's blood pressure, pulse, the sore right shoulder, made sure the sweet tea wasn't spiked, glanced at the medicines to make sure they were being taken. All that took no longer than two shakes of a lamb's tail, and then he was free to track down his redhead.

He found her in the middle of the living room, in a cyclone of a mess.

The Gautier living room was long enough to bowl in, but the kind of place that a kid—especially a boy—was terrified of. All the wall space was taken up with china cabinets and sideboards and casework furniture and breakfronts. Ike couldn't remember the proper furniture names, but basically all the pieces had glass fronts, for the purpose of displaying tea stuff. There were at least a hundred zillion teapots, and even more zillions of little bitty cups and saucers.

It looked to Ike as if a man could break things if he failed to tiptoe…and Ginger had all the glass doors open. Card tables were being set out, and were covered with all those millions of teapots and zillions of the cups and saucers and paraphernalia.

He hesitated in the doorway, thinking that an elephant would be stupid to risk walking any closer. Besides, he wanted a look at her before she spotted him.

Temporarily, she was on her hands and knees, her head almost buried in the lowest shelf of some kind of credenza. She'd scooched her hair back at some point, but strands and curls had done a jailbreak and were tumbling every which way. She'd lost her shoes; her socks were the color of dust, and she was wearing an astoundingly large Clemson University tee—so big Ike figured the garment had room for triplets in the ninth month. Not the sexiest attire he'd ever seen, but it struck him that way.

It was her, of course. She could cover herself from head to toe. She could dye her hair purple. Paint her face in tiger stripes. Wouldn't matter. His blood started sizzling, just from looking at her.

"Hey, Red. Got a minute?"

Her head popped out, swiveled toward the sound of his voice. A brilliant smile of welcome greeted him first...but faster than a snap, the smile dimmed to cordial. The tilt of her head, her sudden careful posture reflected that she wasn't as easy with him as she'd been before. Now there was wariness, defensiveness. Pride.

He knew damn well he'd caused the change.

"To be honest, I really don't have time," she said. "You must have heard about the upcoming tea party—not just because you got an invitation, but because your Ruby's been a godsend at doing a lot of the organizing."

"Yup. I've been hearing about it somewhere around sixty times a day. Ruby was beyond thrilled that you included her in the whole arranging." It helped, Ike mused, that so many people had gotten involved. Hopefully she'd never

guessed that he'd sneaked the idea to Sarah behind her back. He motioned around the room.
"So...what's all this about?"

She sighed. "The whole idea of giving a tea
party was about inviting the community to see
what the Gautier Tea Plantation is about. You
can't give a serious tea party without serv-
ing it with the appropriate china. We have a
museum-worthy collection here. But—I don't
know how—somehow it all got mixed up. The
pattern of teapot should be with its matching
service pieces. Instead, they're all over the sam
hill place."

He didn't give a damn about china patterns,
but she was talking to him. Naturally talking,
the way she had before. "Could you use some
unskilled labor?"

She looked at him, and then laughed. "I
wouldn't mind some help, but honestly, Ike, I
don't think you could handle this."

He didn't bristle. Didn't take offense. Ginger

had ways of putting him down that no other woman ever had, but hey. He had tough skin. "Try me," he said.

She chuckled again, then lifted her hands in a give-in gesture. "You can try, if you really want to. But it's okay to cry uncle and beg off when you've had enough."

He'd do that—cry uncle—on the day it rained moonbeams. "Just tell me what you need me to do."

"Okay. You asked. The china just has to be matched…the teapot with the same pattern service pieces. Each pattern is different, see?" She lifted one to illustrate. "This is called Old English Rose, dates back to nineteen forty. This one is Rose Chinz and this one's Pansy. You can tell them apart, either by looking at the flowers— you know roses from pansies, right? But there's also a signed label on the bottom of each piece."

"This is supposed to be tough?" He figured they'd have this licked in ten minutes flat.

The song on her cell phone temporarily interrupted any further conversation. She tracked down the phone in the front hall, and from what little eavesdropping he could manage, he guessed she was talking to the bank manager.

Once she used Lydia's name, he realized it was a serious call, so he dove into the grunt work. Right off, he realized that sorting the patterns was only half the job. All the dumb dishes would have to be washed. They weren't germ-dirty, just plain old dusty, so he scooped a bunch on a tray and carted them into the kitchen. Piece of cake, he figured.

He rooted under the sink for some dish soap, started filling the basin, then went back to get another load of cups and stuff. Ginger was facing the far window in the living room, still talking—he couldn't make out the words but she didn't sound stressed, so he headed back to the kitchen.

The first cup he pulled from the soapy water

to rinse was somehow broken. Chipped in two places. He looked at it in horror. Then pulled out another cup—and found the handle broken off.

For Pete's sake, he'd been careful. He knew china stuff was expensive. In itself that didn't matter, because he'd replace it no matter what the cost. But to let Ginger think he'd been careless with something important to her?

Guilty as a thief, he wrapped the two broken cups in paper towels and buried them way deep under the trash. He checked the rest of the china in the soapy water. All okay. But he still jumped half a foot when Ginger entered the kitchen.

"That was Lydia Trellace on the phone," she said immediately. She came up behind him, saw what he was doing and foraged for a fresh linen dish towel to dry. "I gave her a proposal for a business plan a few days ago. She called to say that she'd talked to Louella Meachams—that's Gramps's attorney. Apparently I have to go to court—through Louella—to get legal and medical and financial rights over Gramps's life before we can really deal with the farm plan. Lydia said that Louella said that wouldn't be a problem. It just has to be done. She couldn't give me a yes or no on the business plan until then. *Sheesh,* Ike."

"What?"

"You really did a ton of work during the short time I was on the phone."

"Hey, I'm not just a pretty face."

That started her chuckling. "You're coming to my tea party, aren't you?"

"That depends."

"On whether you have patients, or whether you have to dress up?"

"Why would I have to dress up? I could come, and just say that I was fresh from some medical emergency, so that—"

"Nope. No excuses. I'm talking real shoes. A shirt with a collar, preferably white. Dark pants. Haircut. Shave."

He looked at her, aghast.

"I know it's tough, but just like you said, Ike, you're not just a pretty face. You're more than capable of going the long mile."

"That's just mean," he grumped. "A white shirt? I don't think I own a white shirt."

"It's a *formal* tea."

They were bickering like married people, he thought. Her being bossy. Him making out like dressing up for her was an imposition.

He reached for her—not in a big physical way, more like pulling her into his arms for a dance. A slow dance. Married pairs had that advantage. They could use sex to tease their partner into a better mood, to offer a smile, an argument, a sense of fun, a sense of wonder—everything and anything—just not with words. With touch.

She knew that slow dance. Her arms slowly slid around his waist. She tilted her head up. His lips fit just right on hers, no frantic crazy rush, no push, just the kind of soft kiss that evoked memories. He knew her lips. She knew his. He knew exactly what made her eyes close. She knew exactly what knocked him to his knees.

And she did. Knock him to his knees. It was the way she yielded, the way she shared, the things she promised, the things she feared. She opened her heart to him with her kisses. Making it impossible for him to stay sane or sensible or careful.

But then she stepped back, opened her eyes, took a long breath and said softly, "I can't do this, Ike."

"Can't do what?"

"Love you. Be in love with you. When this whole town knows I'm in trouble."

"The town has nothing to do with us." He wanted her back in his arms. And she was close enough to grab her, to pull her in. To claim her again. But the anxiety in her eyes stopped him.

"You've been rescuing me since I got here. And I sure as sam hill needed rescuing. You're a white-knight hero through and through, Ike.

But I didn't know, at the start, that I was going to end up living here. Or that the whole town would be watching us, have eyes on us."

"I couldn't care less."

"I know. You don't care what people say. And I wouldn't normally, but there's a difference between us. You're already a hero for them. So if I stayed with you—especially once my stomach started to seriously pooch out—if you even considered marrying me, they'd assume you were doing the right thing. I'd be stuck with the role of damsel in distress. Only I don't do damsels. I need to build my own reputation, my own way. I need to earn respect, Ike. Theirs. And yours."

"You're nuts, Red. I do respect you."

"I'm not sure of that. I don't know how to be sure of that. You've seen me at my worst, over and over. But I haven't had one chance, even the slightest chance, of being at my best when I'm around you."

He frowned. "Ginger, you don't need to change

anything about yourself, in any way, for me to respect you. I don't know how I could have given you any other impression."

She was so ready with her response. "Unlike all the other doctors in our lives, Ike, you don't put yourself first, ever. You put others first. But right now, I feel I'm lumped in with those others. If you want us to be together, in any way, I want to stand next to you. I don't want to be carried by you."

Well, if that wasn't the dumbest thing he'd ever heard. But when he opened his mouth—not that second certain whether he wanted to talk or kiss her—his pager abruptly went off.

He said hoarsely, "Just hold for one short second." He listened to the message, feeling his gut squeeze acid-tight, looked miserably at Ginger as he punched it off. "It's a kid. Practicing football after school, collapsed out of the complete blue. I—"

"Get out of here. Right now. I don't need the details. Go."

"Ginger—"

"I told you. I totally get it. You need to go. But I need you to understand me the same way. I have to stand up on my own, Ike. I'm not ashamed of making mistakes. But I can pick myself up. I can't be a leaner."

"You're not." But then…damn it. He had to go. "It's a kid," he said again.

As if giving up trying to talk to him, she just motioned him toward the door.

When Ginger climbed downstairs, it was twenty minutes before the guests were scheduled to arrive, and she was more nervous than a trapped mouse. She'd checked everything she could check, prepared everything she could prepare, but she still wanted to give it all one last run-through.

She stopped at the antique mirror in the front hall. Except for the worried eyes, nothing looked wrong about her appearance, at least yet. She'd opted for a soft ivory top and her grandmother's favorite pearls, the knotted single strand. The black slacks didn't button anymore, but no one could see that under the loose top. Subtle makeup was obviously the only choice for a formal tea party, but she'd done her best to make her hair behave with a pair of ivory combs—also her grandmother's.

The toughest thing to shape up had been her hands—all the cleaning had destroyed her nails—so she'd been stuck wasting time on a manicure that morning.

Good thing, since Gramps insisted she wear her grandmother's cameo ring.

That was another lucky omen—or so she was determined to believe.

She traipsed around the downstairs, fretting, checking, fussing.

Gramps and Cornelius were stationed in chairs at the front door, both wearing white shirts and bow ties and shined shoes. They had two jobs: to greet everybody and to behave. They couldn't wait.

Outside—just to make the party more worrisome—a storm hovered over the coast, bringing swirling winds and ominous dark clouds. Ginger turned off overheads, switched on soft lamps in every room. This morning the house had been crazy-busy, with people showing up to help or bring food or participate in any way they could see.

Ginger had been stunned with all the help. She hadn't felt part of the town since she left years ago—she'd believed then that she was leaving, for good. It was startling to hear that folks considered her one of theirs.

Still, she'd set up most things herself—because she needed to. Every space in the downstairs had a function. Every room had different displays. The living room had a station for a formal Japanese tea ceremony, where thick cushions were placed on the floor around a low, round inlaid table. In the opposite corner, an old card table had been judiciously draped with red velvet, where Ruby—when she got here—was going to "read tea leaves."

She glanced out the front door side windows again. No Ike. No one yet. She pivoted around and started prowling again.

The front hall had a massive display of various tea implements—like yixing teapots and infusers, tea cozies and the *guywan,* which was the Mandarin Chinese word for the traditional tea bowl with no handle. A collection of caddy spoons and sugar tongs was displayed on ivory felt. Lydia Trellace had sent over four massive bouquets of fresh flowers. Louella Meacham had literally sent over a man, whom she'd hired to participate in the washing and later cleanup.

By accident, Ginger glanced outside again, just in case she might see Ike driving in.

Still, there was no one—just more clouds and gloom, more thunder.

Well, she had more to check on. Specifically the food—the most terrorizing threat to put together. The kitchen was set up for a breakfast tea—strong black tea, Gautier Breakfast blend—augmented by pastries served with local wild berry spread and a cherry French toast casserole, sliced in small squares.

She'd used the library to set up a traditional afternoon tea—which meant it was by far the most elaborate. There were a half dozen choices of fragrant teas—all Gautier-grown, of course—and then tiers of accompanying food choices: cucumber and cream cheese finger sandwiches, fresh fruit, lemon meringue pie and strawberry tarts, scones and clotted cream. Since she'd done all the last-minute arrangement less than twenty minutes ago, it didn't look any different than the last time she checked.

A flash of lightning in the west made her

jump. It was five minutes to four. What if no one came? Where was Ike? What if they lost electricity?

What else could she find to worry about?

She touched, straightened, fussed. There'd been no place left to set up an evening tea, so she'd just shaken out an Irish linen tablecloth and used some of her favorite teapots with the oolongs and greens. Everywhere she could, she'd set out little parchment cards for those who wanted to know more about tea in general, Gautier tea specifically, or anything and everything about tea customs. Truthfully, all that prep had been fun.

She still thought it was a good idea, for the guests to be able to mill around from setup to setup, not be trapped in any one spot. They could sample as much or as little of anything they wanted. She'd wanted to illustrate what her family had been up to for the last couple hundred years—the teas, the culture, the background and tradition.

Would Ike be proud of her? Or would he be bored out of his mind?

What if everyone was bored?

"Would you stop fussing?" her grandfather grumped. "You look beautiful. The place looks beautiful. There's enough food to feed an army. A big army." He glanced out. "And there we have it. The first car's coming up the drive. And oh, my. I'm afraid there is a pile of cars coming all at once."

She flew to the window. Gramps was right. Cars were turning into the drive, filling every spot on the driveway and onto the side. Naturally, the sky took just that moment to open. Rain came pouring down, sloshing down in noisy buckets. People ran, raincoats over their heads, all laughing as they came inside.

But still no sign of Ike.

A frenzy followed. Thirty people must have

kissed her in the next few minutes as she greeted them and took their wet coats and showed them around. She tried to put Ike out of her mind. He'd never promised to be early. He could have been caught up with patients. And it wasn't as if she needed him. It was just that once, just once, she wanted him to see her as a capable woman and not such a needy one.

The house filled up...and then filled up to nearly bursting. Ginger kept watching the door, not just for Ike but for Ruby—who'd been so excited, and planned to dress gypsy-style, as she played the role of reading the tea leaves.

And just that second she saw Ruby pelting through the door—hustling two strangers with her.

"I was worried something may have happened," Ginger said as she took Ruby's jacket— and got a wet hug in return.

"Something did happen. Ginger, I want you to meet Ike's mom and dad. They just arrived unexpectedly. They're on their way to Charleston, hoped to visit a bit with Ike—but Ike is nowhere to be found. I couldn't track him down. So—"

"I'm *so* glad you brought them. Dr. and Dr. MacKinnon, I'm delighted to meet you!" That was honestly true—although Ginger felt a fresh qualm of nerves after all Ike had told her about his parents.

The nerves didn't last long. Ike's parents were as easy to be with as old friends. Walker MacKinnon was ultra tall, with keen eyes and a tenor voice. June had glossy auburn hair and sharp blue eyes and a gorgeous smile. They were wearing traveling clothes, comfortable shoes— good quality all, but nothing pretentious or fancy.

"Delighted to meet you, too, dear." June took both her hands in greeting. "Thankfully Ruby filled us in that you've been seeing Ike. He never said a thing to us."

Ruby added, "His last patient was at two-thirty. One canceled after that. It's the last I've seen of him."

Walker added, "I hope we're not intruding. We could have waited at Ike's place. He's bound to come home sooner or later. So if we're in the way—"

"Nonsense. I'm absolutely delighted you're here. Please come on in, make yourself at home…."

They were nothing like she'd expected. They'd met many of the townspeople before, were equally friendly to rich and poor, young and old.

Walker admitted, "We don't often call before coming to see Ike. I'm sure that seems odd. But his reality is the same as ours. We're all so busy. So if we get a few days free, we generally try to get away, pop in, see if any of the kids have time for us. If we call ahead, then the kids feel they have to do something, clean, get in food, make a fuss."

"I think it's a great idea. And Ike should be

coming here…so it makes great sense for you to just relax, enjoy yourselves."

An hour passed. Then almost another. Nothing went as she expected. First, because she never dreamed so many people would show up, be so interested. And then because she assumed people would wander around, stop out of curiosity, take in some food, be on their way. Only no one left.

Nothing could possibly have gone better…except for Ike's absence.

And then, just before six, an unexpected visitor arrived who changed everything.

When Ike ushered out the last patient for the day, he hit the ground running. He had a plan—a plan he'd been refining and revising for days. The first step was to unlock the back garage where he kept the Volvo—the truck was his regular vehicle because of Pansy. But the cherished old Volvo was his baby.

His siblings had teased him to no end about Volvos being cars for fuddy-duddies. He'd thought so, too, until riding in this one. The engine purred, she loved curves and she hid a whole lot of passion and power inside the modest exterior. Last time she'd been out, he'd been doing a favor for Tucker...that was a few months ago. She wasn't that dirty, but he still washed and polished and rubbed her to a sheen.

That took longer than planned. Unfortunately, he didn't get back upstairs to his place until after four. He'd never expected to be early for her tea party, anyway. He wanted to be late.

He needed to be late. He wanted everyone to see what he was doing. He wanted to prove—to Ginger, to anyone who happened to look—that he wasn't with her out of kindness or responsibility. He was certifiably, hopelessly in love, desperately hooked, crazy about her.

Next, he took a good shower, did a serious shave, then went the extra mile. He had shirts, but he'd still bought a new white one, one that looked starched and formal. Did the real shoes thing—the kind that actually had to be buffed. Chose pants that weren't jeans or chinos.

That took another heap of time. Who knew he was normally such a slob?

He couldn't find the guy cologne. He knew he had some somewhere, but it was past five now, and he still wasn't done. Then there was the tie issue. He'd worn a tux for his brother's wedding, but otherwise hadn't had a suit and tie on since… hell, he couldn't count that far back.

Still, he had a tie collection at the back of the closet, most dating back to high school or college or Christmas presents from relatives he didn't know. Every single one was ugly, but he had to pick.

By the time he drove through town, hardly anyone was about. Ike figured they were all at Ginger's by now. Ruby had certainly spread the word far and wide, and the whole town had developed an interest in Ginger, in what she was going to do about her grandfather, about the house and tea farm. The coming baby, everyone knew about. All the work she'd done—everyone knew. They knew about her conniving Amos Hawthorne into working for her again, knew about her fainting all over town, knew about the Scuzzball showing up unexpectedly. They hadn't shown up for tea. They'd shown up to show her exactly what she needed to know.

That she was valued. By everyone who'd come to know her.

He wanted to show her that he valued her, too. But in a different way. A very different way.

The next stop was the florist. Naturally they closed at five, but Rhonda White had arranged to wait for him, met him at the back door in the alley. "You know how much this is going to cost you, sugar?"

"I know. I don't care."

"She's going to love it."

"Could you promise that?"

"Don't you worry. She is. Trust me."

It took a huge number of roses to fill up a car with petals. Who knew? And because Ginger wasn't much on pink, he figured he should get coral. Or that's what Rhonda called the color.

After that, he had to stop at the jeweler's. That trip, thankfully, only took a few minutes.

The rain had finally stopped by the time he pulled into her drive. He was shocked at the number of cars—must have been a hundred people inside. The last he knew, Ginger was inviting somewhere around thirty. Ruby'd said that no one wanted to be cut from an invitation so she'd "slightly" altered the original plan. But they weren't all supposed to come. People always canceled.

He parked in front of the porch—double-parked, truth to tell—but he had no other choice. He had to be able to get in and out. Fast.

Chapter Thirteen

Ginger was running on fumes. The party was a success, by any standard she could measure, but her nerves were frayed. It didn't matter if everything had gone wonderfully. The potential for disaster was still very real and all too possible.

She needed the party over, the doors locked, the lights off and the chance to hide under a table where no one could find her.

Instead, the craziest thing kept happening. Guests started to leave...but within minutes of exiting the house, they came right back in. They'd find her, beam, say they "just couldn't get enough" of all the tea lore and "were having such a wonderful time."

She introduced everyone to her father, of course—although she still hadn't recovered from the shock of his showing up. Heaven knew there was no point wasting any surprise on her dad—he'd always come and gone, all her life, on his whim.

He'd walked right in and loved the party. No surprise there, either. Her dad's black Irish looks—blue eyes, cream skin, a thick head of dark hair—were still extremely attractive. He also had charm to spare and a way with the ladies. He introduced himself to everyone as Sean, Ginger's father—as if he was a Gautier by birth. He'd always loved his association to the "landed gentry" status of her mother's family.

Some of the seniors in the crowd knew him from a long time ago, but no one let on there had ever been a problem. Wherever he walked, wherever he stopped to talk, there was laughter—a brash of laughter, smiles, someone being hugged or touched.

Ginger would have survived the visit just fine, except that Ike's parents—Walker and June—quickly strode over to meet him, which was enough to give Ginger a near heart attack. Where was Ike? How come she got stuck with parents on both sides when their meeting had so much potential for disaster?

Her dad could be irresistibly charming, but it was doubtful he could spell *ethic* even with a dictionary, and for certain he had no clue what a responsibility was. Sometime between his first effusive hug and Gramps calling him "John," he'd mentioned being "a little down and out" and that he'd put a suitcase upstairs. Ike's parents had overheard him. So did others.

Which probably meant the whole town knew—in three minutes or less—that the scoundrel was back in town and likely hitting up Ginger for money.

Abruptly she noticed her dad heading for the living room—both Lydia and Louella were in there—which meant there was a risk of some serious harm. She spun on a heel, planning to go after him, when Amos and his wife—who'd just left the party—abruptly reentered through the front door.

Amos's wife looked at her, shot her a big grin and a thumbs up and a wink.

All right. Ginger had no idea why the guests were behaving so strangely, but something seemed to be affecting them when they went outside. It was hard to guess which was the scariest crisis—her father and Gramps's attorney in the same room—or checking out the scene outside. Probably because she was desperate for some fresh air, she decided to whip out on the porch for a minute.

She'd barely opened the door before a swish of silk covered her eyes.

"Don't be scared. It's not a robber or a murderer. It's just your personal kidnapper."

"Ike..." Of course she knew his voice. She felt his hands tying a knot behind her head, trying to secure the silk blindfold. "I don't understand—"

"Everybody's in on it—so you don't need to worry about leaving the party. Ruby's got a whole committee to do the shut-down and cleanup."

"But what—?"

"Nothing's going to happen that you need to worry about. I just need you to come with me, be with me."

She couldn't get his attention. "Ike. Your parents showed up."

His hands stilled.

"And then my *father* showed up, out of the complete blue. I haven't seen him in more than two years."

He finished the knot. "I want to meet him."

"Maybe you really don't." She never meant for him to hear a quaver in her voice. She hadn't realized it was even there. It was just…she'd so badly needed this day to go well. It wasn't about the tea party. It was about feeling competent, competent on the inside. Maybe the lawyer and the banker and everyone else involved would end up saying no to her. Maybe she couldn't save the tea farm. But she needed to give it the lion's try, for the community and Ike—especially Ike— to see that she was more than a young woman with problems, that problems didn't define her.

It all just caused a quaver, that's all.

And Ike must have heard it, because he suddenly snugged the silk blindfold on tighter. "We'll deal with parents another time. Right now we have far more serious priorities. Like your kidnapping. If anything goes wrong with this, I'm afraid the whole town will blame me."

"You're making me uneasy—"

"Good."

"Ike!" Okay, she couldn't help but laugh. "If you think you're kidnapping me, what's the ransom?"

"It's extremely expensive."

"How expensive?"

"All the marbles." His voice…she didn't know what was in his voice, but it made her suddenly shiver. He'd been steering her, hands on her shoulders, blindfold secure, down the porch steps, into wet grass that tickled around her ankles. Probably ruined her shoes, too, but she didn't care.

This was crazy. Goofy. But for the first time in a long time—since they'd made love, she suspected—she felt her heart lighten, not because it was empty, but because it felt full. Full of love and hope both. Full of anticipation. Full of…

Happiness.

She couldn't remember the last time she'd thought that word, much less felt it.

He opened a door, but it didn't sound like the creaky truck door...and suddenly there was a scent. The soft, velvety, unmistakable scent of roses. Everywhere.

"What—?" she started to ask.

"I'm afraid where we're going is a little drive. Under two hours, so it's not that far...but far enough away that no one in town will know where we are. Now..."

Ike was still talking, but she was too distracted to pay attention. He steered her into a car, the passenger seat—but a passenger seat that had been adjusted to a lie-flat position. When he closed the door—obviously to come around to the driver's seat—he'd secured her seat belt.

He started talking again, the moment he entered the driver's side, but temporarily her senses were consumed with textures and scents. There weren't just roses in the car. There were rose petals. Heaps and heaps of them. Her passenger side was a mattress of velvet, unbearably soft petals, the scent alluring and unforgettable.

"I knew this wouldn't work," Ike was saying, "if you were worried about your grandfather. So I set up a group of people to check in on him, be with him, from Sarah to Amos to Lydia—all of them volunteered. Then I know you're worried about the business plan, the loan…and that you have legal issues you're waiting to hear about, like medical and legal powers for your grandfather, so that you can pay his bills, protect his interests. Louella had a word with me yesterday—you know her, she wouldn't give away your secrets or cross any ethical lines. She just made it bluntly clear that you won't have trouble getting what you needed. And again, on your grandfather, old Doc Brady—the doctor I replaced? I'm sure you knew him from when you were a kid. Anyway, Doc Brady and Stephie, his retired nurse, will both be on call for the next few days. No strangers. No one your grandfather doesn't already know and feel comfortable with…."

She pulled off the scarf and turned her head to look at him. Really look at him. She'd never seen him nervous before, but he was. His fingers were drumming on the wheel, couldn't keep calm. And there was a rose petal on his shirt, another in his hair.

He looked darned silly with a rose petal in his hair.

"Where we're going is Whisper Mountain. The MacKinnons have always had a place there. Actually, we have a couple of the places, but there's a cabin up on the highest ground. Pretty rustic, so don't be expecting too much—but we'll be alone. No anxieties, no intrusions, no interruptions. My sister Rosemary's been hanging there for quite a while—since she broke off an engagement—but she's taking a month off right now, doesn't need the place in any way. She's got Pansy, if you wondered, so don't be worried about that, either—"

"Ike." She wasn't sure he was going to stop talking. If he was even capable of stopping. As far as she could tell, he hadn't even stopped for breath.

He glanced at her, noticed she'd taken off the silk blindfold and shot her a worried look— but his gaze was drawn immediately back to the road. The pavement snaked in wildly sharp curves, too dangerous for a driver to look away more than seconds.

"There's a legend about Whisper Mountain," he said. "You'll laugh, it's that corny. But there's a legend that the mountain whispers—really whispers. But the only people who can hear it are those in love. I haven't a clue how the story got started, but even my great-grandparents—"

"Ike," she interrupted again, this time in a soft, low voice.

This time he heard her. Shot her another quick

look, worried look, but had to return his attention to driving.

"Now don't object until you've seen it," he urged her. "It may be rustic, but it's not—"

"Ike, I don't need to hear a mountain whispering to me. I already know. I love you."

"Just go with—what?"

"I love you. With all my heart," she said simply.

He jerked the car so hard she feared they were diving straight down a mountainside. But Ike, being Ike, pulled them both out of trouble. For a couple seconds there, though, he was in an extraordinary fast hurry to stop the car.

Ginger woke up slowly, feeling more luxuriously rested than she had in weeks, just wanting to snuggle deeper into the pillow and blankets. For long moments, she didn't open her eyes, just savored the scents and sounds and textures around her.

Warm sunlight blessed her closed eyelids. The smell of pines and cedar drifted close; even closer was the crackle of a cherrywood fire, the softness of a down pillow, the whisper of cinnamon and roses in the air.…

Only…

She didn't have a down pillow. There were no pines or cedar trees anywhere near her bedroom, and she couldn't imagine a reason in the universe for how or why she could be smelling cinnamon.

But her eyes popped open when she caught the scent of roses. The scent of roses was real for her in every way.

She shot up on an elbow, wide-awake that flash-fast, and took in the rest of the unfamiliar room. Rustic cedar beams. A slanted ceiling. The four-poster bed she'd slept in was bigger than a boat. Across the room, a stone hearth had a grate full of sharp orange embers, and a tidy stack of fresh cherrywood on top. The top blanket covering her was a handmade quilt—it had that heirloom sort of look—and the wood floor was varnished, shiny as a mirror.

Nothing was familiar. Even remotely.

Except for Ike.

He was reading, from a giant-size upholstered rocker by the hearth, his stocking feet up on an ottoman. Maybe he'd slept, but it didn't look it. He was still wearing the white shirt he'd had on yesterday. He'd pushed off shoes, at some point brought up a tall glass of something, and his chin sported a fresh crop of whiskers. Now, too, she could see drifts of roses, one on a sock of his, some on the floor, some on the blanket…a regular Hansel and Gretel trail, leading from her.

To home.

Ike was home.

"Hey, kidnapper," she murmured. "Did you sleep at all?"

His head shot up. He immediately put down the book, and once she could see his face, she knew the answer. The intense lines on his brow, the gray shadows under his eyes…no, he hadn't slept.

But his answer was a simple, "I got enough." He didn't move, but looked her over as intensely as she'd studied him.

"What time is it?"

"Around one."

She lifted her eyebrows. "How could it be one? There's sunlight outside—"

"That's because it's one in the afternoon, lazy bones. Which is partly why I didn't try to sleep. You needed—really, really needed—a block of rest. I got you up a couple of times—pregnant women invariably can't make it many hours without a bathroom run. But I think you were half in a coma, didn't really wake up even for that. There's some food downstairs. I made cinnamon rolls. Well. At least, I followed the directions on the container. And there's eggs. I can either do an omelet, or scramble up a bunch. You have to be hungry."

"I am. Near starved." She crooked a finger, inviting him closer. "I just need to talk to you about a couple of things first."

"I can talk from right here."

"No. I don't think so. I have a problem that I need your help with." She hadn't thought up a problem yet, but she knew what motivated Ike. If he thought she needed him, he'd be there faster than jet speed.

And as expected, he pushed out of the rocker immediately, came forward immediately, sat on the bed immediately. But Ike—who always moved with a lanky, boneless rhythm—approached with a careful, robotic stiffness...and she hated the wary expression in his eyes. He carved a seat on the bed near her side, but he didn't attempt to touch her.

She was pretty sure he wasn't afraid she had cooties. So it had to be something else.

"I have a feeling you were watching me sleep for quite a while," she said.

"Maybe. I just didn't want to leave you alone in a strange place. I knew how badly you needed the rest."

"I did. But watching someone sleep has to be unbelievably exciting…on a par with watching grass grow." That won almost a smile. Not a full smile, but a teensy untensing of all those taut muscles.

"Maybe I find watching you sleep unbelievably exciting."

"Ike?"

"I'm right here. What?"

"Come clean. What's wrong?"

"What could be wrong?"

There happened to be four pillows on the giant bed. She flapped his head with one of them. And there. She caught the ghostly but unmistakable hint of a real grin.

"It's possible," he said delicately, "that you

might wake up from a sleep this sound and forget what you said to me last night."

"You mean…about loving you? About being in love with you? Specifically about being crazy in love with you?"

He looked out the window, then back at her. "I never thought I'd hear you say those words. The love words. But as much as I wanted to hear them…I was kicking myself."

"Kicking yourself why?"

"Because I was afraid my plan, what I thought was my great, romantic kidnapping plan, could have backfired. I suddenly realized that you could have felt…pushed. Pressured. Because so many people saw the car, the rose petals, me dressed up like a stranger."

"Wearing a tie, even."

"Wearing a tie, even."

"And without Pansy."

"And without Pansy. Ginger, I didn't want to put you on the spot. Didn't want to make something hugely private to me—to us—to come across as something to be shared in public. It wasn't like that. What I wanted was for you to know—for everyone to see—that I was in love with you. That I wasn't with you because of the baby bump or your grandfather or the tea. It was about you. Being the woman I wanted to fill up the car with rose petals for. Do you remember what you told me?"

"Which thing?" Her voice was thick, from hearing what he'd planned, how he felt.

Hearing her vulnerable man lay himself bare.

"You said that respect was something you had to earn. You didn't expect it for nothing. But you wanted to earn that respect—from me. From everyone."

She pushed back the covers. Even though she'd loved all the cuddling warmth, suddenly she didn't need the blankets. Didn't need the pillow. She just needed to be closer to Ike. "I do feel that way. That respect has to be earned."

"So that's where the whole rose petal idea came from. Because you were pregnant, you were afraid the people in town—neighbors, friends—would assume I was with you out of honor or responsibility or some idiotic nonsense like that."

"Yup. That's exactly how I feel about honor and responsibility."

He didn't seem to hear her teasing attempt at humor, just went on. "So I wanted them to know—I wanted you to know—that I loved you over the top. Loved you in ways that have nothing to do with the baby or honor or responsibility or because you may or may not need someone. I never thought you needed anyone, Ginger. You're strong as a rock. You are a rock."

"Man. Is there an insult in there? Because I feel I should have a chance to brush my hair and put on some makeup if you're going to insult me."

"Quit it, Red. I need you to hear me."

The look in his eyes made her heart ache. "I wasn't trying to make jokes, Ike. I'm listening."

"You *are* a rock. That's the point. People do respect you. I respect you. You proved that from the first day you came back to town. You lit into anyone like a firecracker if you believed they were a threat to your grandfather. People just assumed that you came back because you had to—but that you'd take five minutes with Cashner, close down the place and lock him up in an institution."

"Yikes. That hurts. That anyone thought that of me."

"They hadn't seen you in a lot of years, Ginger, except in passing. They only knew you as a girl. Your mom had been dead a long time. And while some saw your father now and then…"

She nodded quickly, sadly. "I know…they assumed that I had some of my father's blood. I've had that misconception bite me in the heart before. It's partly why respect—real respect, earned respect—has always been so important to me."

"Well, from the day you came home, you threw off anyone's preconceptions like that. You were nothing like your father. You came out fighting for your grandfather's rights. For doing whatever you could to give him the best life he could have. And you sure argued with anyone who tried to stand in your way."

"Okay, okay. Enough about me." If he kept talking, conveying how proud he was of her, how he perceived the things she'd done, she was afraid she'd cry. And dagnabbit, she never cried. "Let's get into one of the real problems here. What are we going to do about your reputation, now that the whole party saw you kidnap me in the car with all the rose petals?"

He sighed. "I'm afraid you'll have to marry me. I'm afraid the kidnapping…well, I didn't think of all the consequences. My practice will likely be shot. My patients will all think I've cracked, that the commonsense M.D. they knew must have become deranged and derailed somehow. And I can't even defend myself, because it's true."

"You think?" she asked tenderly.

"Ginger, I'm crazy for you. The baby's no burden. I'd love to be her father. Or his father. I'd love to give you a whole basket of babies, both genders…" He hesitated. "But to be honest, I'd prefer little girls with gorgeous eyes and terrible tempers."

"You want *ornery* children?"

"I do."

"Oh, Ike." Clearly, she had to save him. No one else would ever realize he was in such bad shape but her. She pushed back the last of the covers and more or less dove. Not as if she were diving into a pool or a lake, of course, but still, launching herself at Ike, on Ike, so that he simply had to fall into the mounds of down covers and mattress.

He went down. And stayed down. Like a fighter who knew when he was licked—which Ike most certainly was.

It killed her that he'd been so unsure. That Ike, who had so much natural confidence and common sense, could be lain low by worries about her. Of course, Ike wasn't so self-aware. He still didn't realize that he was just as driven as the other doctors in his family, to be there for others in need, to stand up...particularly when normal people would be running for the nearest exit.

While she had him prone, she dipped down and kissed him...no teasing, no playing, not anymore. This kiss conveyed the real thing—that her being in love with him was the real thing. No pretense, no caution, no holding herself back. This was it, a plain old naked kiss, coming from her heart, eyes closed, pulse thumping like a rickety hiccup, love spilling out a deluge of desire and need before she could even try to get it under control

Eventually, at some point, she let him up...seeing as they were both gasping for breath. The tension in his muscles was completely gone, except for one specific area.

The wariness in his eyes had completely disappeared, too.

He got it—that she was going to save him just as zealously as he'd saved her.

Still, being Ike, he had to push. "Would you mind my taking a turn at being on top, Red?"

She wanted to laugh, but her heart seemed to spill a more honest answer. "Any time you want, lover."

When he kissed her this time, she closed her eyes and felt awash with wave on wave of fierce tenderness.

There was so much they had to sort out and fix and work with. But not now. Right now Ginger had no doubt that she and Ike could conquer the world together...as long as they had each other.

* * * * *